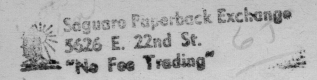

Harlequin Presents...

Other titles by

VIOLET WINSPEAR
IN HARLEQUIN PRESENTS

VIOLET WINSPEAR

the kisses and the wine

Harlequin Books

TORONTO • LONDON • NEW YORK • AMSTERDAM • SYDNEY • WINNIPEG

Harlequin Presents edition published August 1973
ISBN 0-373-70518-2

Second printing August 1973
Third printing November 1973
Fourth printing July 1974
Fifth printing August 1974
Sixth printing April 1976
Seventh printing June 1976
Eighth printing February 1977

Original hardcover edition published in 1973
by Mills & Boon Limited

Printed in U.S.A.

CHAPTER ONE

DASH the car! It was small and red and secondhand, and she had bought it in the Portobello Road, and her friend Cass had said at the time that it was definitely the sort of vehicle that would go wrong in the most inconvenient place and leave her stranded somewhere in the middle of southern Spain.

Everyone had thought she was crazy making the trip alone, but for once in her twenty-two years Lise had made up her mind to take a holiday that would be organized by herself alone, her dear but bossy brother and his wife left at home while she toured the twisting, up-and-down roads of this fascinating country, stayed the night at whichever inn took her fancy, ate cheese, bread and fruit by the roadside and didn't make a formal journey of it as Audrey liked, guide book and museum catalogue in hand all the time, and a concern that the beds be well aired and the water free of germs. Audrey was a dear but a worrier, and Lise had felt the need of a carefree, solitary holiday for a long time. It worried Audrey that she was not yet engaged to be married, and Lise liked to have a game with her rather earnest sister-in-law by telling her that she had joined the female liberation movement and planned to live a free and emancipated life, with no demanding male to run her life.

But the truth was that right now Lise would have appreciated the masculine knowledge of cars and what made them stall on a mountain road with nightfall coming on. Lise lifted the bonnet and stared at all the complicated bits and pieces of machinery inside the car that looked so neat and sure of itself when the bonnet was closed. She had set out so eagerly on her *aventurilla*, as the Spanish called it, and the little car had been so good until now. She slid into the driving seat and tried once more to get some response from the engine, but all that resulted were cranks and grinds enough to wake the dead, and Lise began to feel that she had arrived at a place unknown to the living.

All around her stretched the corniche road into the hills, and all was strangely silent, as if even the birds had flown off and left her alone with her predicament. She thrust a hand into the pocket of her suede driving jacket and took out a bar of nuts and raisins. She was feeling peckish and the inn at which she had planned to stay for the night was still some miles up the mountain slope. She guessed it was the tough going which had finally made the car call a halt, and with a shrug Lise ate her way through the chocolate bar and firmly told herself that it was no use getting into a panic. Someone was bound to come along soon, for she knew this road to lead to a township, and she could then ask for assistance, or a lift to the nearest garage. This part of Spain wasn't so benighted that there wouldn't be a mechanic available to put the car right. After all, she had to be in Madrid by the fifteenth to see if there was a possibility of working in that *salon* which Franquista had recently opened.

Lise was an exceptionally fine needlewoman and for some time now she had worked for a well-known fashion house in London. Franquista had visited the establishment about four months ago and when she had been shown some of Lise's work she had said at once that there would always be an opening for the English girl in the *salon* she was planning to start on the Avenida Felipe in the busy heart of Madrid. It was her meeting with the Spanish couturier which had given Lise the idea for this holiday. It had seemed an excellent way for her to make the break from her brother's household and establish herself as a young woman of independence. She only joked with Audrey about entire liberation, but what she truly wanted was the adventure of working in another country and meeting people as vivacious as she had found Franquista. Bob and Audrey were inclined to treat her as if she were one of their children, and though she loved them for their concern and kindness, she was really old enough to take care of herself and make a career elsewhere than in London.

She leaned back in the driving seat and listened carefully to the stillness, hoping to have it broken by the oncoming sound of another car.

She glanced up at the sky and saw the first faint glimmers of starlight. Night was falling and she had never been so alone in her life before. She wasn't exactly nervous, but now those tales of primitive Latins began to seep into her mind; those warnings from her friend Cass, who had visited the Costa del Sol last year, that Spaniards had cave-men ideas about women and believed them to be pawns of pleasure rather than people.

Lise had laughed at the time, but now as she glanced round at the dark, towering shapes of the mountains and breathed the wildly perfumed air, she sensed an atmosphere of menace and beauty that might indeed be a background for ravishment of a lone virginal traveller like herself.

Nonsense, she chided herself, and then she stiffened in her seat as very distinctly she heard the rushing of wheels on this silent road, the oncoming velocity of a very fast car, suddenly roaring round the bend beyond which she was parked and seeming to aim itself directly at her lights

7

and the small bulk of her car. There was instantly a terrific screech of wheels as the driver braked and came to a halt in a cloud of road dust only a yard or so from the small red open-top.

Because for the past four months Lise had been busy learning the Spanish language she understood the expletive which the other driver used to describe someone who parked on the bend of a narrow road in the middle of the *sierras*.

In the flare of his headlamps Lise saw his face, and the dark Latin force of the features, combined with his anger, made her heart race with panic. He looked the picture of fury, and she was a young woman all alone with him. As much as she needed help, she prayed that he would expend his anger and drive on, but abruptly he threw open the door of his long, powerful car and strode to the side of hers.

His swift, cutting Spanish was way over her head, and though she had an inclination to cower away from his high and mighty anger, she tilted her chin and waited for a pause in his speech to explain that she had not parked here to admire the view but had trouble with her engine. All at once he stopped berating her in his incisive Spanish and stared down at her with narrowed dark eyes.

'Of course,' he snapped out the words in perfect English, 'only an outrageously confident British tourist would park in such a position and dare fate to bring disaster upon her. You do realize that if I had not applied my brakes my car would have hurtled yours over the side of that precipice?'

She followed the direction of his lean, sweeping hand, and it was so annoying that he should be so right. 'My car stalled, *senor*. I did not park here on purpose—'

'I see.' He swept a look all around her. 'You are alone? You have no companion?'

8

She swallowed dryly and hated to have to admit to this bad-tempered brute that she was all alone. But even before she answered him, she saw from the black joining of his brows that he comprehended fully her aloneness and her youth, spotlighted by the headlamps of his car directly upon her. She met his eyes and defiance flared in her light grey eyes, giving them a crystal-like quality.

'As a driver yourself, *señor*, you know how these things can happen, but I won't detain you as you are so obviously in a great hurry. I can wait for another car to come along, with a driver who might be good enough to give me a lift to the nearest garage.'

'Parked as you are, *señorita*, he could well give you a push into the nether regions. Are you out of gas?'

'No, the gauge is still registering. I think something is amiss with the engine.'

'And so you planned to sit here in the hope that a good Samaritan would come to your aid, eh?'

'Is such a hope impossible in Spain?' she flared, her temper ignited by his Latin scorn of what he considered female irresponsibility. 'I suppose Don Quixote is out of fashion in this day and age!'

'It is a point to be argued, *señorita*, but not at this precise moment. This is not exactly the busiest road in Spain, so what if I had not come along? Don't tell me you would have ventured out on the mountain road in search of a garage?'

'I'm not that foolish,' she rejoined. 'I'd have spent the night in the car and hoped to find assistance in the morning.'

'You refuse to consider yourself foolish, but if you want my opinion, *señorita*, you are asking for trouble driving alone in this region of the country, without any real knowledge of your vehicle, and palpably unaware that it grows extremely cold in the mountains as the night advances. What if a wolf came along?'

'One with two legs?' she asked flippantly, and could not help but shrink back as the tall Spaniard leant down against the open side where she sat and gave her the most explicit look of her life. It spoke volumes. It said she was an impudent child, totally devoid of common sense, and very much in danger of being hoisted from the car and thoroughly shaken. It even said more . . . that he was someone not accustomed to being sauced by a mere female of the species.

'I am strongly tempted to drive on and leave you to face the dark, cold night alone,' he said grimly. 'It really cannot be wondered at that your country has no Don Quixote. His kind of gallantry would be wasted on headstrong females who brag of being self-sufficient, yet who lack the grace to ask politely for help when they find themselves in need of it. Well, young woman, do you want my help or do you wish to give way to your impulse to tell me to go to the devil?'

Lise felt strongly the grip of that impulse, but she also felt the touch of the night wind against her neck and it was cold, and she had only a thin laprobe in the car to protect her against the elements.

'I – I do need help,' she admitted, and never in her life before had it been so difficult for her to request it. 'Could you have a look at the engine and perhaps do something that might make it possible for me to reach the nearest village?'

'I am afraid I am in a hurry and cannot afford the time to tinker with a car engine in the half-dark. You had better come with me. Come, out of the car, and bring with you your belongings.'

'You will take me to the village?' She couldn't help but feel a sense of relief. 'I am grateful, *señor*.'

'The nearest village is out of my way,' he said curtly. 'I will take you where you can spend the night, and in the morning someone can be sent to deal with your vehicle. Come!'

It was a most definite order and Lise felt that if she didn't obey it he would drive on and leave her alone without even a backward glance. Inwardly fuming at his autocratic manner, Lise climbed out of her red car, looked at it and took her suitcase from the boot. She had been travelling light, wearing a trouser suit and several changes of gay cotton shirts and nylon underwear. On her feet she wore kid driving-shoes, and she put their flatness down to the fact that she felt small beside the Spaniard as he escorted her to his Jaguar. He opened the passenger door and she slid inside, feeling at once the warmth and comfort after the smallness and austerity of her own car.

He took the seat beside her and slammed the door. He turned to her a moment, took her case off her lap and tossed it to the wide back seat with a sardonic sort of carelessness. 'You might as well be as comfortable as possible,' he drawled. 'Would you like a laprobe?'

'*Gracias*, no, *señor*. Your car is very comfortable and I am grateful to you for giving me this lift.'

'You really should be grateful to providence that it was I who came along and not some rogue who would take advantage of your ineffable innocence.' His voice was as smooth as the action of his car, taking the uphill road as if it was borne on wings, leaving behind them the gay little car which now looked oddly pathetic. Lise glanced back, and he said at once that he would arrange to have it towed to a garage. 'If you were a Latin girl you would be named Inocencia for certain. What bravado, to tour Spain all alone! And what sort of parents have you to allow it?'

'I'm not a child,' she said stiffly. 'I am over twenty and I have managed very well up until now.'

'Over twenty, eh? I would not have taken you for that.'
The car sped swiftly through the night, its headlamps showing how precipitous was the road, like a narrow ribbon en-
circling a dark gorge. Now and again Lise shot a glance at
the man beside her and she couldn't help but admit that he
had a most striking profile, the brow, nose and jaw carved
with the precision which was truly Latin, with a well-
groomed cap of black hair above the strong brow. A commanding face to match his voice, she thought. The face of a
grandee!

'Do I meet with your approval?' he asked suddenly, and
she flushed vividly and was glad that the interior light wasn't
bright enough to reveal the hot colour that came and went in
her cheeks; the proof, had he need of it, that she wasn't
entirely at ease with tall, dark, imperious men.

She didn't reply to his sardonic question and neither of
them spoke again until the Jaguar had put several miles
between them and the place where she had stalled. But at
last, because she had thought he was taking her to the nearest village so she could register for the night at the local inn,
she was forced to ask him where they were going.

'Are you nervous of me, then?' he asked, a softly mocking
note in his voice.

'No – as a matter of fact I'm rather hungry and I thought
we'd have reached the nearest inn by now.' Her reply was a
defiant one, for how could she help but feel nervous of a
perfect stranger with hair and eyes as dark as night, and a
manner which betrayed his opinion of her as a little fool
bent on getting into trouble. The fact that he was well-
dressed, well-spoken, and the owner of an expensive car, was
no guarantee that he wasn't one of the Spanish wolves Cass
had warned her about. Cass had said that most Spaniards
liked to dress well, and most of them had a certain air of

distinction which could fool a girl. Lise tightened her hands together in her lap and for the first time in her life she was at the mercy of wondering what she would do if this man should stop the car and reach for her with those lean well-kept hands with a gemmed ring on the small finger of the left hand.

Her heart nearly stopped as in that moment they turned a bend and he stopped beside a tall pair of gates. Even as a little cry of protest clamoured at her lips, he pressed on the horn and made it blare loudly until suddenly a light went on and revealed a sort of gatehouse, with a squat stone tower, at one side of the road beyond the closed gates. A door opened and a figure, struggling into a coat, came running to open the iron gates.

As they clanged open the long car started up again and they swept through the aperture on to the gravel of a drive. Lise caught a glimpse of the gatekeeper's face and she thought he looked a bit scared, or was he merely startled after being woken from his sleep by the blare of the Jaguar's horn? She hadn't realized until now how late it had grown, so that most people would be in bed, or preparing to go there, especially those who lived in the hilly regions and had none of the distractions of town life to keep them from their bed.

'Would you be as good as to tell me where we are?' she demanded. 'I only came with you because I thought you were taking me to the nearest village, but this seems to be a private driveway—'

'It assuredly is,' he agreed. 'The driveway to my house—'

'Oh – how dare you!' she broke in on his explanation. 'I – I should never have trusted you! I knew from the first moment I looked at you that you were devilish!'

'Just as I knew you were foolish,' he said crisply. 'It is

said that first impressions are usually the correct ones, but I would ask you to reserve judgment of my house until you see it in the morning light. You might very well take it for Bluebeard's Castle in your present state of mind – and possibly your hunger. I assure you that I can offer you a far more comfortable bed than the local innkeeper, and also a far tastier supper.'

'And what am I expected to offer in repayment?' she snapped, and the words were out of her mouth before she could suppress them, and they revealed very clearly the trend of her thoughts and her fears. Oh lord! She closed her eyes in momentary horror. What if he were a Spanish big-shot, with not the least intention of harming her; what if he had a wife to whom he would relate her remark and make of it a highly amusing joke between them? Lise wished to heaven that caution was part of her make-up, but she had always been rather impulsive, to the despair of Audrey, who swore that it was Lise's tendency to speak her mind which kept young men from wooing her with serious intention.

Lise sat as still as a statue in the deep veloured seat of her rescuer's car and waited for him to berate her, or on the other hand to amusedly admit that he hoped to have a little fun with her.

'And now do you feel better,' he asked, 'having got off your mind the inevitable question – asked by the innocent and the experienced alike?'

'Put yourself in my shoes,' she muttered. 'You allow me to believe that you're taking me to the village, and instead you bring me to your house. If you are a married man, I doubt if your wife will be pleased about providing supper and a bed for a total stranger.'

'In my household I am the master,' he said suavely. And in that instant he brought the car to a halt and the sweeping light of the headlamps revealed a structure that took away what breath Lise had left after his autocratic statement. Stone steps mounted to a great oaken door, and above that rose the frontage of a castle, topped by a cluster of square turrets and a long, indented balustrade surrounding them, and the entire building loomed and rambled and gave off an aura of ancient beauty and history. Lights winked here and there behind the windows, and when Lise stepped from the Jaguar she breathed the scent of all sorts of plants and flowers, stealing over the stone walls and hanging in pale and dark clusters.

'This – this is where you live?' The words broke from her, and a little gasp came from her throat as he came to her side and took her by the elbow. His fingers gripped her, right through the suede of her jacket, and there was a sudden tension about his face as he gazed down at her.

'I have done you a favour, *señorita*, now I ask you that you reciprocate – please, don't jump in that silly way! I am not about to ask you to honour me with your undoubted virtue! It is that I am in rather an awkward situation – for the past year I have pretended to have a fiancée in England, a pretence that was necessary in order to stay my grand-mother's hand. I have a great affection for her, but I will not permit the old matriarch to choose my wife for me. She did this for my father, but she will not do it for me, and to save argument I have invented a wife-to-be whom I met, so she believes, while on a business trip to England. A little dip-lomacy is worth a thousand arguments, and I would be most grateful if you could pretend to be that mythical fiancée of mine. For just a few days, *señorita*. Before my grand-mother can embarrass me by announcing to one and all that her ward, Anastasia, is to be my bride. This was threatened a year ago, and exactly to this day I promised to produce my own choice of bride. If tomorrow she is not forthcoming, the Condesa will place me – deliberately – in the awkward situation of accepting or rejecting her ward. The girl is lovely. I don't deny it – but I will not be coerced and forced into marriage merely in order to provide the next generation, as my father was. It is legendary that he and my mother – an Iberian girl straight from a convent – were never happy together, but all the Condesa cares about is that the family name be passed on, and in her estimation I have been too tardy about this.'

He paused at this juncture and the look he bent upon Lise was dark and compelling, and his grip was even more forceful as the great door of the castle opened and light shafted down the steps.

'Allow me to introduce you as my English fiancée and I promise I will give you anything you desire in return. The young have many wishes, and this situation must appeal to a girl with your large and world-wondering eyes. I came to your rescue, now you can come to mine.'

'But the situation is entirely different,' Lise protested. 'You are a total stranger to me.'

'You allowed that stranger to carry you off in his car. I could have murdered you, but all I am asking is that you bring a small pretence to life. In return you can have a new car to replace the one which is probably, under the bonnet, put together with shoe-string and gum. In a new car of excellent make you can go anywhere without the fear of breaking down and finding yourself at the mercy of a dark stranger.'

'Am I at your mercy?' She could feel the bite of his fingers as she spoke, and she could see the demanding glitter of his eyes. A manservant was coming down the steps of the castle towards them, and she knew that this was the most fateful moment of her life. She even believed that this Spaniard would break her arm if she did not submit to his outrageous wish. Her large eyes pleaded with him to let her go, but with abrupt determination he drew her close against his side and he fiercely whispered:

'What is your name? Come, tell me!'

'Lise,' she said breathlessly. 'Lise Harding.'

'Mine is Leandro de Marcos Reyes.' His breath fanned her cheek as he imparted to her the impressive name, and then the manservant had reached them, and she heard him welcome home to the *castillo* the Señor Conde.

Her head reeled and she went weak as the Señor Conde encircled her with his strong arm.

'Blasco, I wish you to meet my fiancée,' he said in very deliberate Spanish. 'I should have telephoned ahead so that a suite could be prepared for her. She is very hungry, however, so while we eat supper together her rooms can be aired and made ready. She will have the Dove Suite which belonged to my mother.'

'*Si, señor.*' The manservant cast a swift look at Lise, who had never been so close to fainting in her life. Everything was suddenly so unreal . . . everything but the arm that gripped her as she and the Conde de Marcos Reyes mounted the steps towards the open door of this castle that dominated a Spanish mountainside.

'Y – you must let me go,' she said, and she tried to pull away from him, only to find that his strength was as audacious as his suggestion that she play the part of a fiancée he had invented.

'I cannot,' he said. 'You are now committed, Lise.'

She automatically corrected his mispronunciation of her name, but thought how appropriate that he should make it rhyme with 'lies'. 'You called yourself the master,' she scoffed. 'It hardly seems masterful to me, to be scared of being forced into a marriage you would find fettering to your independence.'

'In this one particular case love is my master,' he said, in clipped tones. 'The Marcos Reyes family has diminished to just two people, my grandmother and myself. I happen to care for her, but I will not have that caring used by her to force me into marrying a pretty creature of her choice merely for the sake of making babies – to put it bluntly. If the Condesa wished me to be the normal sort of Spaniard she should not have sent me to an English college. I not only learned to speak your language, *señorita*, but I learned to like my independence, and I will not take on the yoke of marriage until I am ready to do so, least of all with a young girl reared to the idea that women are made for only one purpose. To put it bluntly, I wish to marry a woman of the world, but the very idea would kill the Condesa. You, who look so young and unworldly, will fit in very well with my plan to keep the Condesa from throwing her ward at my head. She will see at once that you have good teeth, skin and hair, and that will be sufficient for her.'

'Like a – a filly,' Lise gasped. The whole event had taken a mad turn as far as she was concerned, and suddenly she began to laugh and just couldn't stop. Hands gripped her shoulders and shook her. Dark eyes looked directly down into hers, and deep within them burned a flame of danger . . . a signal that he would have his way and she had better give in to him, or get hurt. Tiredness swept over her, an inability to fight his dominance made her want to weep.

'I think I hate you,' she said fretfully.

'You may hate me, so long as you don't reveal it,' he rejoined. 'It is essential that the Condesa believes you to be this girl I found in England, for it does her no good to have those continuous arguments with me. She has a heart defect, you understand. And she is very much the Latin woman who likes to have her own way. On this matter I remain adamant. I choose my own wife!'

Lise could only gaze at him in bewilderment, there beneath the lights of the great hall into which they stepped as he spoke. 'I – I must be dreaming,' she said. 'No one in reality would suggest such a thing – that a pair of strangers pretend to be engaged. It would never work, in the first place, and I would feel an absolute fraud and be bound to give myself away. I'm no actress, *señor*.'

'But you are a young woman of spirit, who came to Spain looking for adventure. I offer you one. Are you too afraid to be a Doña Quixote?'

In the strangest way this description appealed to her, and she found herself reluctantly intrigued. She had often longed to tilt at a windmill, but up until now her life had run along safe and regular lines. She hardly dared to think of what it would mean to act the part of fiancée to this tall, commanding Spaniard, with eyes so dark the pupils shone like jets at the centre of them.

'It's all very mad,' she murmured. 'A lot for you to ask in exchange for a bed and a bite of supper.'

'I'm not forcing you,' he said, and he took his hands away from her and left a curious feeling of coldness in place of where his touch had been.

'Aren't you?' she said, and she looked at him very gravely, and saw for the first time that he was the best looking man she had ever met in all her life.

No! The good teeth he had remarked on clenched over the word. She wasn't so romantic and female that she was going to be led into this masquerade because a man happened to be . . . well, devastatingly good-looking in a dark, hawkish way, standing there in a perfect fitting pair of grey slacks, a smooth dark jacket that fitted him like a glove, and with a cravat of dark blue silk tied loosely about his brown throat. He was about thirty-four or five, and he looked as if he had always liked twisting women around his little finger.

No, he wasn't going to twist Lise Harding around his finger. She glanced wildly at the open front door, beyond which the manservant was mounting the steps with her suitcase, its red leather bright against his alpaca jacket. As she ran towards him he paused and looked rather startled. Then Lise gave a little cry as the Conde leapt after her, swift, silent and intentional as a panther, and caught hold of her.

'*Amada*, you must not be nervous of meeting my grandmother,' he said in Spanish, so the servant would understand his words. 'As I told you before, *pequeña*, she will be so delighted that I have decided to marry you that she won't mind – after the first shock – that you are so unsophisticated and so very different from Latin girls.'

'Let me go!' Lise twisted in his grip, and at once, with a flash of white teeth at the man carrying her suitcase, Leandro de Marcos Reyes swept the reluctant, struggling girl up into his arms and carried her effortlessly and purposefully across the hall of his castle, making for an oval door set deeply in the solid white wall, against which stood enormous Moorish-looking pots aflame with scarlet azaleas.

'You must have a glass of wine to settle your nerves, little one.' And though he spoke with a smile, his grip was like steel.

Lise was helpless in that grip and she knew it as he thrust open the oval door and carried her into a room where a log fire glowed in the fireplace and played its shadows over walls lined with deep red leather and masses of books.

It was such a warm, richly comfortable room after the darkness that surrounded the castle, and the wind blowing down from the sierras, that Lise was captivated against her will. She was lowered to her feet and held for a brief moment against the smooth material of the Conde's jacket and she was acutely aware as never before in her life of the magnetism that certain men could exert. He held her and drew her towards the fireplace, a great oval of stone alive with flame and warmth, and with lean hands he pressed her down on a great leather footstool and smiled to himself as he went to a mahogany sideboard to pour wine from a crystal carafe into matching glasses on long stems.

Lise noticed that he smiled . . . like a man who had once again made a woman surrender to his autocratic will.

'In Spain we say that a good sherry is the king of wines.' The Conde handed down to her a glass of the wine he had poured, and Lise took it because she really did need something to steady her shaken nerves. She had never dreamed that by accepting a lift from this man she would land herself in her present predicament. If she insisted on leaving the *castillo* she had no way of knowing how to reach the village, and she could tell from the Conde's face that he had no intention of taking her there. Also the wind had risen out there in the night; she could hear it howling in the wide chimney of the fireplace and the very sound made her incline towards the glow of the burning logs. Leandro de Marcos Reyes had planted himself in front of the fire, looking so tall because Lise sat on the pliant footstool that she had to look all the way up at him, to where he rested the rim of his wine glass against his lips . . . lips, she had noticed, with both a hardness and a certain sensuality to them.

'Drink your wine and it will make for you a feeling of *felicidad*, *señorita*. The wine of the grapes grown at El Serafin are said to have the sun of the slopes in them, and also a little touch of the snow that resides upon the peaks of the *sierras*. Come, you mustn't hold on to the glass as if I have given you hemlock to drink.'

'You called this place El Serafin,' she said. 'Is that the name of the castle or the region?'

'The castle is the region, *señorita*.' He smiled quiz-zically, as if at her innocence. 'All the land that stretches around us at this precise moment is land owned by the Con-desa and myself. The castle stands on a rocky niche, with the mountains towering above its turrets, both grim and splendid, half gold and half stony-grey. The blue jacaranda tree grows in our courtyards where we capture the sun, but when there is a storm our rooftops are often pelted with hailstones. The situation of the castle is said to dictate the character of the Marcos Reyes family and we are said to be both hot and cold-tempered people.'

'I see.' Lise obeyed him, now, and drank some of her wine, which had a taste of fruit and fire in it and was in-stantly warming. 'Are you warning me that when you lose your temper there is hell to pay? That I would not enjoy the experience and would find it easier to give in to your – your incredible proposal?'

'Were you not told that we in Spain take very seriously the maxim that one good turn deserves another? Here at the castle you will be far more comfortable than at a mountain inn catering for pedlars and travelling troupes of gipsy dancers. Our beds are warm, clean and large, and our cook is the best in the region. Now you must be feeling very hungry and I cannot allow that a moment longer.' He strode to a bell-pull affixed to the wall near one of the overflowing bookcases and with his hand upon it he quirked a black eyebrow at Lise. 'Do you fancy *empanada*, which is a hot pie packed with appetizing meat, onion and peppers? It is a favourite dish of mine and Florentina always has one pre-pared when she knows I am on my way home. I should men-tion that the family business is concerned with fabrics of every sort, from the finest velvet to the sheerest silk, and from the softest suede to the strongest leather. I am the director-general of our manufacturing organization in

Madrid and I am home at the present time for the birthday of Madrecita. In a few days' time she will be eighty years of age, and the gift she expects from me is a *novia*. What harm, *señorita*, is there in a little deception? When you return to England you can forget all about me, but for these few days bear with me – make me this good turn, eh? Think of it in this way. You will be saving a man from a marriage of disaster – the act of a real Doña Quixote.'

'You mean the act of a Doña Infeliz,' Lise rejoined.

'You think I take you for a simpleton?' He jerked on the bell-pull, and then gave Lise a sardonic smile. 'It was a little foolish of you to drive alone in Spain, which is said to be the land of devils and saints, and though I think you a bit of an innocent, I don't regard you as simple. I believe you to be a rebel, *señorita*, who is running away from a certain situation in England which has become trying for you. I read in your eyes a certain defiance – am I correct?'

'It's really none of your business.' She stared down into her wine glass, for it was unfair that he should have the advantage of being so worldly that he could read her dilemma in her eyes.

'Is it a young man?' he asked, and under her lashes Lise could see him approaching her across the deep golden carpet, his feet encased in hand-tailored shoes, and his long legs made even longer by the narrow, well-tailored trousers. He had, she thought, a silent, animal tread, as if he were stalking her and would trap her beyond escape.

'Do you imagine that I am going to unburden myself to a perfect stranger?' Lise gave him an indignant look.

'I shall have to know one or two things about you, if we are to convince Madrecita that I have known you for a year. You must tell me about your parents—'

'I have no parents. They're dead, and my brother who is ten years older than I has always looked after me. He's mar-

23

ried and has a family, and all I want is to make a life of my own. There it all is in a nutshell, but if you think I'm going through with this *novia* business then you are mistaken, Señor Conde. You have no right to ask, or expect such a return for your – your generosity in bringing me here for the night. I don't doubt that everyone else jumps as if whipped when you crack an order, but I'm a British tourist, and I'll pay you for my night's bed and board!'

'You amuse me.' A smile flicked across his lips. 'You come alone to Spain, yet you have so little knowledge of the Spanish character. How dare you think that I would accept payment for my hospitality!'

'How dare you assume that I would jump at the chance to play your fiancée,' Lise shot back at him. 'You must consider yourself highly irresistible, and so accustomed to exerting your *droit du seigneur* that it comes as a shock when a mere female refuses to do your bidding. I tell you I refuse—'

As her words rang out the door opened and a stout woman in a spotless apron and dark dress entered the room, looking at Lise with large eyes over the contents of the tray she was carrying.

'*Señor*, I bring your supper,' she said, and she carried the tray to a circular table set in the window space and she was still staring at Lise, taking in her fair tumbled hair and her blazing grey eyes . . . the very British contrast which she made to the dark, lean, autocratic figure of the Conde de Marcos Reyes. 'The good Blasco told me that you had brought with you your English novia, *señor*. I hope the young lady will like my *empanada*, which tonight has chicken included with the veal. It is all nice and hot and I recommend that you both sit down at once to eat it.'

'*Gracias*, Florentina.' He gave his cook a warm smile, and once again he directed at Lise an intent look, which seemed

24

to fill her clear eyes with his Latin darkness. 'Well, *amada*, shall we eat supper together? I can assure you that Florentina is the best cook in the whole of El Serafin. She is herself from Galicia and has brought with her all the cookery arts of that famous region, and she will not forgive you if you permit her *empanada* to grow cold.'

He held out a hand, the left one on which gleamed the wide band of his ring, set with an emerald that shone like a small malevolent eye. Lise tensed herself for contact with his hand, and then his fingers had gripped hers and she was drawn to her feet. She looked up wildly at his face, and it was so adamant that it might have been carved from tawny teak; his lean fingers gripped hers and he made her walk with him to the table where Florentina had set out the plates and cutlery, and removed the speckless linen which had covered her pie. Lise saw that it had a decorative golden top to it, into which was baked the family coat of arms.

'Our escutcheon,' he said smoothly, 'is a hawk, a tower and a lily. It makes a pretty picture, eh?'

He drew out a chair for Lise and as she sat down she caught the aroma of the pie as Florentina sliced into it. Lise was only human and she weakened to that delectable smell of meat, gravy and sliced onion.

'It smells heavenly,' she said, and when Florentina glanced inquiringly at the Conde he smiled and translated the English words. The plump cook, with glistening black hair drawn back from a rather nice face, broke into a smile that showed several golden teeth which gave her at once a roguish look. She broke into quick Spanish, which Lise could not take in, in her present state of mind.

'Florentina thanks you for the compliment,' said the Conde, shaking out his table napkin to spread it on his knees. 'She says that I am fortunate to have a *novia* who appreciates good food.'

Lise bit her lip, for he was pushing her further and further into the quicksands of his deception. She wanted to protest to Florentina that she was not his *novia*, had never been so, for his existence had not been known to her until he had come upon her out of the darkness . . . like Lord Pluto himself! Lise sought for the Spanish words that would explain the truth to his cook, but they had fled for the moment, and left her mind blank of the language she had been studying for the past four months.

She gave a start as the door closed behind Florentina . . . she was alone with Leandro de Marcos Reyes and there was nothing she could do for the moment but tuck into the *empanada* . . . which tasted as delicious as it looked.

CHAPTER TWO

THE *castillo* which towered above the region of El Serafin was a truly splendid example of Spanish architecture, preserved down the years and kept in good structural condition by the de Marcos Reyes family. Set there against a background of mountains and forest it looked exactly right, and in daylight it could be seen that its stone walls were a dark tawny shade, with the turrets pointing into the blue sky, graceful, proud and strong.

It was the kind of place which had always housed a proud and determined set of people, and Lise was very aware of this as she came in from the veranda where she had been standing and met again the dove-like eyes of the portrait over the fireplace. She had slept deeply in the bed with the crown-shaped canopy and long silk drapes to enclose it from draughts, moths or shadows. It had a carved headrest, a long stool at the foot of it, and that portrait on the wall of the woman who had used the room long ago.

Lise still found it hard to believe that Leandro de Marcos Reyes had been born of such a gentle-faced creature. She had such a quiet beauty as she sat there in the golden frame, the blue-grey folds of her velvet dress falling about a slim, girlish figure; her only jewellery apart from her marriage ring a jewelled crucifix on a gold chain. Her dark hair was looped back in a madonna style from her brow, and Lise remembered what he had said last night . . . his mother had come from a convent to be the bride of his father, but the marriage had not been a successful one.

It had been, Lise thought, a case of a dove mating with a hawk . . . and the result had been a man who swooped on whatever took his relentless fancy.

She, a thoroughly respectable and law-abiding British girl, was the latest victim of that fancy, and she felt like a fly in a gilded web as she gazed around the bedroom to which she had been brought last night, and in which she had slept the deep sleep of the exhausted.

Now in the morning light she was wide awake, and she was curious, and in the grip of a reluctant admiration of her surroundings. There was no doubt that never in her life before had she slept in such a beautiful room, set within the tower of a Spanish castle. She had realized that she was housed within a tower when she had gone out on the veranda and found it semi-circular and poised above a deep drop to the courtyard below. She had gazed over the stone parapet and there below had gushed and bloomed the blue jac-arandas *he* had talked about during supper in that book room lined with rich Cordoban leather.

She gazed intently at the portrayed face of his mother and tried to find in the gentle features some resemblance to Leandro de Marcos Reyes, but there was none, and she came to the conclusion that he must look like his father. Or perhaps his grandmother, that formidable old lady who insisted that he take a bride and ensure the continuation of the Marcos Reyes line. Lise didn't doubt that he would do just that, in his own good time, but in the meantime he meant to conciliate the Condesa by producing a fake fiancée, and he had picked on Lise to play the part.

Suddenly it was as if the pictured eyes of his mother caught and held her own; they were large, reflective and brown, and they seemed to hold two deep wells of sadness, as if she had tried with all her soul to make her marriage a happy one. What had gone wrong? Had she been too spiritual for the man she had been chosen to marry? Had she been too gentle of heart, with not enough fight or challenge in her to please a proud, hard, passionate Spaniard?

Gazing at the face that was the shape of a heart, dominated by the beautiful eyes, Lise felt certain that she had hit upon the truth. How could a dove hope to please a hawk ... and the present Conde was afraid of the same kind of marriage for himself. He had said very emphatically that he wished to marry a woman of the world ... the kind of woman of whom his grandmother would be unlikely to approve, for she would not be the kind that a matriarch could dominate, as she more than likely dominated her ward. A lovely girl, he had said, but not the one he wished to marry.

The eyes of his mother seemed fixed upon the young, spirited, upraised face of Lise Harding, and there seemed to be a sort of pleading in those eyes.

For what was she asking? The heart within Lise's breast seemed to race ... oh, no, she could not stay here to play a part in a masquerade which could lead to all sorts of complications. She was a stranger to these people, and it was wrong of Leandro de Marcos Reyes to accept as a stroke of destiny their meeting on that mountain road; to see in her a fortuitous answer to his dilemma.

She turned away from the portrait of the woman in grey-blue velvet and saw that the sun through the windows was lighting up the apartment and revealing its beauty. There was a wonderful lidded vase on a small carved table of shiny black wood, a striking contrast to the enamelled surface of the vase. In a recess of the wall there was a display of lovely, delicate fans of lace, ivory and paintwork. The wallpaper was patterned with delicate leaves and small golden lilies, and there were wall-lamps with little gold parchment shades. All the furniture was of dark, richly carved wood, but the sheen to it made it seem silken, and beneath her bare feet Lise could feel the thick, smooth carpet.

She didn't wish to respond to the room, the portrait, or the castle, but she had a romantic nature, and perhaps deep down in her heart she had hoped to find herself in a place like this when she had come to Spain. The golden beaches of the Costa del Sol had not appealed to her and she had made no attempt to visit the popular and fashionable places. As her gaze took in each article of this bedroom she felt the urge in her fingers to touch and caress. Her eyes held a grave and questioning look as they dwelt on the curving walls ... did she regard herself as a prisoner of the Conde's castle? Did it really lie in her power to escape from the man who had brought her here ... and did she really and truly wish to escape?

Her thought was interrupted, the answer to it suspended as there came a tap at the bedroom door and it was opened to reveal a young, dark maid carrying a breakfast tray.

'*Buenos dias, señorita.*' Even as the maid smiled, she flashed a quick look over Lise, who immediately guessed that the staff had been busy talking about the '*inglesa novia*' and as a flush swept over her face she saw a little knowing gleam come into the Spanish girl's eyes. She thought Lise was flushing because she was under observation as the bride-to-be of the dark and handsome Conde. The girl wasn't to know that Lise was feeling as guilty as if she had been caught stealing something.

'The *señorita* will take her breakfast in bed?'

Lise had been wandering about in her robe, but she didn't wish to return to bed and she indicated that the tray be placed on the table that stood between the windows that opened on to the veranda.

'*Si.*' The girl did her bidding, and as Lise took her seat at the table the sun flared through the windows and tangled itself in the fair disorder of her hair, which had almost a marigold shine to it, but was of a soft, fine texture which made a formal hairstyle an impossibility. All she could do was comb it and clip it away from her eyes, and it was this informal brightness of her hair which gave her the illusion of being so young.

'What is your name?' Her rather uncertain Spanish had returned and she was so pleased with herself that she smiled and looked far less anxious and trapped.

'I am called Rienta, *señorita*. I am to be your maid and when you have finished your food I will return to help you with your toilet.'

'But I don't need any help.' Lise gave a startled laugh and took the top off her boiled egg. 'I'm not used to having a maid and—'

'My orders come from the Señor Conde.' Rienta looked a trifle shocked that his *novia* should say she was unaccustomed to being helped to bathe and dress. 'It is promotion for me, *señorita*, and I do hope you will not refuse to have me for your maid. The *señor* would think that I do not suit you—'

'Oh, it's nothing personal,' Lise said hastily. 'I'm from England, as you know, and we don't have maids any more – oh dear, I can see that you are anxious about your job. Very well, Rienta, if the *señor* insists that I have a personal maid, then I suppose we had better comply with his imperial wishes.'

Lise took a bite of her egg and it wasn't until she caught the astounded widening of Rienta's eyes that she realized what she had said. She had not only been mildly imprudent, but she had more or less allowed it to be understood that she was his English fiancée. And the Spanish girl, with a delighted smile, was leaving her for the moment to return to the kitchen with the news that she was acceptable to the *novia* and from now on would have a more important and congenial occupation in the household.

'Rienta!'

'You require something else, *señorita*?'

Lise looked into the dark and sparkling Spanish eyes and the words would not come . . . she couldn't say what should be said and see bewilderment, perhaps scorn come into the eyes that looked at her and liked her. The sun flowed warm through the windows from the Spanish sky, and Lise had been assured that the masquerade would only last for a few days.

She smiled at the girl. 'Please tell Florentina that my breakfast is very nice.'

'*Si, señorita.*' The girl gave an old-fashioned bob which was not out of place in castle surroundings, so far away from the informalities and rather dull activities of Lise's life in England. 'We all wish to make the *señor*'s *novia* feel at home.'

The door closed behind Rienta, and Lise bit her lip as she buttered a piece of toasted bread. Well, she had committed herself and must now play her part as the Conde's mythical fiancée. She bit into her slice of toast and thanked heaven that Spanish couples were far less demonstrative than English couples, and were not allowed to really give way to affectionate feeling until the actual wedding took place. It would have been an impossible situation had she been expected to act the ardent bride-to-be, hanging on his every word and glance, and almost faint with longing.

All he required, thank heaven, was her English presence at the castle in order to prevent the Condesa from handing him her ward as his future bride. If he openly refused the girl, he would make it seem that she was not good enough for him, and Lise believed that Latin people took very seriously these real or imagined slights to their matrimonial desirability. A Latin girl openly refused by a *conde*, a man of title and position, might be doomed to spinsterhood, which in Spain was about the most awful thing which could happen to a girl . . . so Lise had heard. But if he could produce a *bona fide* fiancée the girl named Anastasia was let off gracefully, his grandmother was conciliated for the time being, and Lise spent the latter part of her holiday as a guest at a picturesque castle.

Lisa finished her breakfast with an orange, probably plucked from one of the trees down in the courtyard, and as she tasted the sweetness of it, she hoped that nothing bitter would spring from this masquerade between herself and Leandro de Marcos Reyes. She glanced again at the portrait of his mother, but there was nothing there of his dark and penetrating eyes, his firmly sculptured nose with the tempered nostrils, or his mouth which combined the sardonic with the passionate.

Lise was unsurprised that she recalled his face so vividly. Once seen it was a countenance hard to forget. 'O Spaniard, of lightning and fire,' she thought, as she finished her coffee.

Rienta returned to the Dove Suite, and Lise submitted to the attentions of a maid for the first time in her life. Her bath was run for her, and when she entered the bathroom she couldn't suppress a gasp of admiring astonishment. It had a glazed shower, a toilet in its own blue alcove, and set within a lining of mirrors was the sunken tub. It was extremely sybaritic to have belonged to a bride who had come from a convent, and as Lise slipped into the scented water, she wondered what had been the reaction of that dove-like creature when she had arrived here to be the wife of a man she had never met before the wedding. It seemed a barbaric practice to Lise, and a little shiver ran through her as she thought again of the present Conde.

Thank heaven she was only a make-believe *novia* and had no need to fear him as a real lover.

When Lise climbed out of her bath, Rienta was waiting to wrap her in a large soft towel, and there was in her eyes an expression of wonderment as they dwelt on Lise's slim white shoulders.

'Are all English people so lily-skinned?' she asked. 'Even the men?'

Lise broke into a smile. 'My brother Bob wouldn't care to be called lily-skinned, but I suppose our men haven't the tawny-gold look of your Spaniards. When they toast themselves in the sun they go a sort of tan colour, which I must admit is rather attractive, but the trouble is it soon fades away. In England we don't get days and days of sunshine.'

'You mean it is cold, like the tops of the *sierras*? I should not like that, *señorita*, and I understand why you came to Spain to be a bride.'

'Oh, but I shan't be marrying the Conde just yet.' Lise flushed again and hastened into the adjoining bedroom. 'I—I have merely come to El Serafin to meet the Condesa. She may not approve of me.'

Lise was suddenly aware that she would have to learn to be more composed each time her supposed relationship to the Conde was mentioned. At the moment her fingers were shaking as she slipped into her lingerie, and she could feel how her cheeks were burning as Rienta looked at her. But there was a smiling indulgence in the Spanish girl's eyes, as if she thought that Lise was shy. She had unpacked Lise's suitcase and now she stood looking at the everyday apparel she had taken from it. The cotton shirts, and the spare trouser-suit, and the single dress of white, sleeveless piqué.

'Is your other luggage to be sent on, *señorita*?'

'Y-yes,' Lise fabricated. A visiting fiancée would be bound to have more clothes than she had brought with her on her driving holiday, and if the mythical luggage failed to arrive it would be assumed that it had got lost in transit. 'I'll wear the blue shirt and the fawn trousers, and save the dress for this evening.'

'Yes, *señorita*.' But Rienta obviously disapproved of the trousers as she handed them to Lise. Her manner said quite plainly that the Señor Conde wore the trousers around the castle and that was as it should be.

'Trouser suits are very fashionable in my country,' Lise explained. 'They are so comfortable and casual.'

'The Señorita Ana wears trousers only when she rides, and then it is the Cordoban style, the divided skirt, you understand, with a short jacket and the hard-brimmed hat. She looks very charming in the outfit.' As Rienta said this she looked at Lise with a hint of injured patriotism in her glance, as if the members of this household, and very possibly the residents of the region, had expected the Señor Conde to become betrothed to a Spanish girl.

Lise felt again the fraudulence of her position here, and she was about to rush into words that would end it all when there was a sudden demanding rap on her bedroom door. Rienta had been brushing Lise's hair, and now they both stared into the mirror at each other, and the words which Lise had been about to say were hushed like birds at the approach of a hawk. The accelerated beat of her heart told who was at the door and a sense of panic seized her. She didn't want to see him . . . she wanted an end to this game they were playing before it became dangerous.

'I had better open the door, *señorita*. It may be the *señor*.'

Each nerve in Lise's body told her that it was he, and she sat tensely at the dressing table as Rienta went to the door and opened it. He stood there looking every bit as tall and demanding as she remembered him from last night, only this morning he was wearing a white shirt open at the throat, breeches and long boots, and in his hand he carried a whip.

'Good morning,' he said in English. 'May I come in? I see that you are dressed.'

Lise rose from the dressing-stool, and she felt the flick of his eyes over her hair, which hung loose and straight to her shoulders. She raised a hand to it, defensively. 'Good morning, *señor*. How the sun shines! I'm still taken by surprise at the quick warmth of the Spanish sunlight.'

'You do look a trifle – surprised,' he said, and there was a slight smile upon his lips as he turned to Rienta and told her to run along because he had one or two things to discuss with his *novia*. This time he spoke in Spanish, unaware as yet that Lise had recovered her shaky but workable knowledge of the language. Rienta bobbed and hurried away, and he closed the door of the bedroom so he was privately enclosed with Lise whose nerves seemed alive with tiny barbs under her fair skin.

'You slept well?' His eyes left her face and skimmed the canopied bed, and that smile at the edge of his mouth seemed to deepen, as if it amused him to think of someone as slight as herself ensconced in that great double bed.

'Amazingly well,' she said, 'considering that I had so much on my mind. I must have been tired out.'

'You must indeed, *señorita*.' He came further into the room, treading with that silent sort of danger over the carpet, the ebony handle of his riding-stick dark against his breeches. In daylight she saw the hint of mahogany in his skin, and the steel-smooth movement of muscle in his forearms, rippling to join those in his chest and shoulders. That hint of the graceful animal allied to the natural hauteur was more than disturbing, and Lise felt herself moving back from him, until she was brought up short against the veranda windows. Her hair blazed nimbus bright as she stood there, with wide grey eyes fixed upon his darkly handsome face.

'What is the matter?' he asked. 'Are you afraid that I expect you to react like a real *novia* when we are alone together?'

'I understood, *señor*, that Latin people display decorum in all matters relating to their – affairs. Is it quite proper for us to be alone like this?'

'In your bedroom, do you mean?' There was a gleam of diablerie in his eyes, which even in daylight were so dark as to be almost black. 'In Spain we have not yet reached that stage of permissiveness so prevalent in your own country, but we have discarded the use of the *duenna* to a great extent. There was a time when if I had wished to speak alone with my *novia*, an older woman would have been present, perhaps behind a curtain, to make sure I did not presume to take my bride's virtue before the taking of our mutual vows. Which must all seem very much like the Middle Ages to a young woman of the world who drives about a strange country all on her own.'

'Meaning that if I had had someone with me, I would not have found myself in my present predicament.'

'Is it such a predicament?' He quirked a black eyebrow, and then gestured around the room with his riding-stick. 'Do you not like the Dove Suite? Do you not find it far more comfortable and attractive than a rather bare, whitewashed room at a *parador*? Did you not enjoy your breakfast, and having a young maid to wait on you? Come! You would hardly be human, or truthful, if you denied that you found none of these things pleasurable.'

'It's the deceit involved, *señor*. I'm not used to it.'

'Then let us not call it a deceit but an actuality.' He tossed his whip to the bed, pushed a hand into the hip pocket of his breeches and withdrew from it a small box. Before opening the box he glanced at the portrait of his mother, and then as if something in her eyes reproached him, he took Lise by the elbow and led her out on to the veranda of the suite, where the sun was flooding over the gracious ramparts of the *castillo* and over the masses of trees and plants that from this height gave the appearance of green velvet spread over the land.

Lise slipped free of his fingers and leaned against the parapet, which had a lacing of iron sewn with rambling creamy flowers.

'Do you know what they are called?' He gestured at the flowers, and she shook her head. 'They are the Chaste Jasmine which grows in our Marcos Reyes soil with a wonderful fervour. The plants were brought with my mother from the convent at Castile, and they have bloomed here at the castle ever since. They are strangely symbolic of the sort of woman she was. She was far too lovely for her family to agree that she become a nun, but that is what she wanted. However, the alliance with my father was arranged, settled, and she was not an independent British girl, but an Iberian daughter of stern and unyielding parents. She came here as a bride to a man, but she left her true self behind in the Convent of the Blessed Heart. She is there now—'

'But you said—' Lise stared at him in astonishment mixed with a certain sense of shock. 'You told me that only the Condesa and yourself are left of the Marcos Reyes family.'

'This is true, *señorita*. My mother was never truly a Marcos Reyes and when I came of age, and inherited all of this, my father then being dead, my mother returned to Castile and re-entered the convent. She is happy there and is doing with her life what she always felt she was meant to do. I don't blame her for the choice she made, but it means that I can see her only now and again. It also means that the Condesa and I are rather closer than might have otherwise been the case, and she is not a gentle soul like my mother. We probably have more in common. A lot of pride, temper, and self-will, and we clash on any of the main issues of life

38

and at the forefront is my tendency to be cautious in the taking of a wife. I know the kind of wife I want. The Condesa thinks she knows the kind of wife I need.'

He paused and opened the small square box and he gazed intently at the contents. 'What is your own interpretation of love, *señorita*? I feel sure you have thought about it, even as I feel certain that you have not yet been in love with a specific man.'

'I–I haven't thought all that much about it,' she denied. 'I have been more concerned with making a career for myself – that was why I came to Spain in the first place.'

'You hoped to work in Spain?' This time she had surprised him, and as she met the deep-set, alive and searching dark eyes, she felt the delayed impact of his question about love. Heavens, here she was . . . this moment was all too real, and never in her life before had she been so sensitive to the physical attraction of a man . . . in fact she was feeling this strongly for the very first time, and she clutched at the mundane in order to offset the unusual.

'I have to be in Madrid by next week, *señor*. I intend to apply for a position in the sewing room of Señora Franquista's new *salon* which she has opened there. I have met her and—'

'You have met Franquista Valdes?' The Conde looked astounded. 'When was this, *señorita*?'

'When the *señora* visited England and several of the fashion houses in London. I was working at Nelson King, which is one of the best couturier *salons* in London, and Franquista came there to see a show and to meet some of the staff. I was introduced to her because I had sewn the wedding dress which was the highlight on the show, and she said that if ever I wished to work abroad I was to get in touch with her. I thought a lot about her suggestion, and when I fully realized that I was a bit fed up with the well-established routine of my job in London, I decided to accept the *señora*'s offer of a job at her fashion house in Madrid. I was combining my holiday with my decision to apply for the job; seeing something of Spain in order to be sure that I wished to work here.'

'And are you sure?' Leandro de Marcos Reyes was studying her with eyes with glittered with interest and curiosity.

'I think so. It will make a great change for me to work among new surroundings, always supposing that Franquista has not changed her mind about employing an English girl in her sewing room. She was kind enough to say that I had skill and talent.'

'Did you like her?' he next asked, and it seemed to Lise that tiny brilliant lights came alight in the depths of his dark eyes, and she wasn't sure what caused them. Whether it was amusement at her earnestness, or some sort of personal emotion. She thought of the striking, camellia-skinned face of the fashion designer, the silken precision of her coiffure, the tiny dark mole beside her mouth which emphasized the fullness of her red lips. Lise had thought her very beautiful in a worldly, Latin way, and she had heard of the scandal attached to her name in Spain. She was one of the few Latin women who had ever been divorced, and that was because she had been married to a South American whose birthplace had actually been the Argentine, where the divorce laws were not quite so strict and where he had applied for and been granted his divorce from his Spanish wife.

Lise knew that in Spain itself the beautiful Franquista was considered a very sophisticated and worldly woman . . . and looking now into the glinting eyes of the Conde, Lise had the most astounding thought. He had spoken last night of wanting to marry a worldly woman . . . was it possible that he had been thinking of Franquista Valdes, the daring divorcee who would be totally unacceptable by the Condesa de Marcos Reyes as the wife of her grandson!

'Do you know the Señora Franquista, *señor*?' Lise just had to ask; she had to find out if her suspicions were justified, because in a strange way the masquerade he suggested would seem less objectionable if she actually knew the strength and sincerity of his motive. Recalling the warm and vital personality of the Spanish couturier, Lise could at once believe that this very vital man loved such a woman and would find it impossible to put in her place the young, pretty, unworldly ward of his grandmother, who had probably hoped all along to bring about such an alliance.

'Yes,' he murmured, moving in his lithe and silent way towards Lise, 'I am acquainted with Franquista Valdes. She buys from us the materials for her fabulous and highly-priced garments.' He reached Lise and took firm hold of her left hand. 'It is the accepted custom in my country for a *novia* to be given a betrothal bracelet of gold, and I have always held the rather cynical view that the Spanish girl likes to be given a bracelet because it has more gold in it than a ring. However, as you are English I am going to put upon your hand a ring which once belonged to my mother and which she left in my care when she returned to Castile. Her own family had ancestors who were Castilian knights, and this ring has been handed down the years to many different brides – *dios*, don't jerk your hand in that way, *señorita*. You and I know that we play a game which will never become a true reality, but if you wear this ring, then Madrecita will be convinced that I mean business.'

Lise could not move her hand as he held it, she felt both the living steel of his touch, and the golden grip of the ring as he slipped it on to the third finger of her left hand, following the English tradition of engagement rather than that of Spain, as if in this way he did not commit his true self,

41

the Spaniard who when he became truly engaged to the woman he loved would follow all the Latin ways and enclose her curvaceous arm in a wide golden bracelet.

The grey eyes of Lise gazed incredulously at the ring he had placed upon her finger. The golden setting was intricate as the Spanish character, and at the heart of the ring burned a dark sapphire, so densely blue and beautiful that it seemed almost alive, sending out shafts of flamy colour as the sunlight found the gem and added its rays to the glory of the sapphire.

'No!' The word broke from Lise. 'It would be blasphemy!'

'You don't like it?' His hand gripped her shoulder and seemed to bruise her bones. 'What makes you use such a word as blasphemy?'

'It's a love ring!' Lise would have wrenched it off her hand, but he quickly forestalled her by grabbing hold of her right hand. '*Señor*, take it off, please!'

'Don't be a little fool,' he said curtly. 'Anyone would think that it was burning you. It is just a ring, a token to convince the proud, obstinate old lady whom I love that she cannot dictate to me as she did to my father. I know what she plans to do, to announce to the newspapers in Madrid that I am to marry her ward. Your presence here, and the presence of that ring on your hand, will stop her from making an announcement I should either have to repudiate, or accept, and either way would be disastrous for Ana, as we call her. A repudiation of her as my future wife would be like a public slap round the face; an acceptance of her as my wife would ensure that neither of us would ever know a real moment's happiness.'

He stared down at Lise. 'For a marriage to work there has to be not only *simpatia*, which is a subtle joy of the senses meaning rather more than happiness, which on the whole is a somewhat childish emotion, but there has to be a driving urge to be together for always. If this is absent, then it is a waste of time for a man to marry. He might as well have his affairs and remain free to give most of his energies to his work. I asked you a short while ago if you had ever thought of what love might mean – I ask you again, *señorita*, and your answer may explain to you, yourself, what I am attempting to explain. I like Ana. She is a pleasing child, but when I say this does it sound as if I love her unto death?'

Lise could only shake her head. 'Surely if you explained to the Condesa—'

'Madrecita is only concerned that a grandchild be placed in her arms before she dies. Ana is young, healthy, nice-looking, and in the estimation of my grandmother, reared in the old tradition, that is sufficient for a man. If he wishes for the foolishness of romance, then he must seek it outside the home, but the home is for the founding of a family, and in her words I have virility enough to build up the Marcos Reyes clan until it is once again a sprawling, robust castle community.'

'And you don't wish for that?' Lise murmured.

'Let us say I am an emancipated Spaniard, *señorita*. I wish to make and have joy – I never once in my boyhood and adolescence saw a sparkle of joy in my mother's eyes. She wasn't a cold woman, or too spiritual that she couldn't have been won with real love. She was a woman who had been married to a man for the same reasons that my grandmother would have me marry Ana. Would you, Lise Harding, wish to be a wife of the body rather than the heart?'

'No—' She quickly shook her head. 'I'd hate it.'

'Which means that you have given some thought to love and what it should mean.'

'I – suppose so.' Her lashes swept down, shielding her eyes from the invasion of his gaze. 'If one can say, "your words are my food, your tears my wine," then I imagine that could be called love.'

'Hunger and a little cruelty, eh?'

'Yes – love seems to me to have an element of ruthlessness in it. I – I can't visualize it as a gentle emotion. The making of love isn't gentle, is it?'

'You have made love with a man?' There was a sudden cutting edge to his voice, and Lise gave him a quick, almost shocked look.

'Heavens, no! But I'm not an innocent who believes in fairy tales, *señor*. I have heard of passion, and I do know that babies aren't plucked with the strawberries.'

A smile edged his lips, and then he lifted her hand and studied the sapphire ring upon it. 'Have I convinced you that you will be doing a quixotic action if you wear this for me?'

'Are you certain, *señor*, that I can convince your grandmother that we knew each other in England? Are you sure she will believe that I am the type to capture your interest, let alone your heart?'

At once he ceased to study the ring and to study Lise instead, as she stood there in the golden Spanish sunlight, clad in a blue cotton shirt and slim-fitting slacks, her hair like pale shining rain about the fine-boned, almost elfin features of her face.

'You make quite a contrast to the Latin girl,' he said. 'Madrecita will assume that it is your difference to which I am attracted, but it is the *fact* of you which is important to me. When she sees you, an end will be put to her little trick to force my hand with regard to Ana, and when we part it can do no real harm if I continue the pretence a while longer in your absence.'

'When you say a while longer,' Lise looked at him rather angrily, 'do you mean you are waiting – expecting your grandmother to—'

'*Dios*, no!' Now it was his turn to look angry. 'With care and no violent upsets Madrecita will live another decade. No, I am thinking of what will inevitably come to pass between Ana and a certain friend of mine when Ana meets you and realizes that I have no intention of making her my wife. There will be no need for words or explanations. Latin girls are reared to the idea that they must marry, and I have been for the girl the nearest male object for a long time now, ever since her parents died in a train disaster and she was brought here to be raised by my grandmother, who had been godmother to Ana's mother. You understand?'

Lise nodded, and could very well understand how an impressionable young girl would, as she grew up, develop romantic ideas about the darkly handsome Conde. Lise also believed that the girl would be far more disappointed than he casually supposed, when his mythical English fiancée came suddenly to life and was introduced to her, wearing the sapphire ring which had been his mother's.

'Did you never attach a name to your make-believe *novia*?' she asked dryly. 'Or a description? And why pick on England to have been the place where you supposedly fell in love?'

'To answer the last question first,' he gazed down at Lise with a sardonic expression in his eyes, 'Madrecita knows too many people in Madrid and other cities of Spain for it to be sensible of me to invent a Spanish *novia*. She would have demanded the young woman's family name and all sorts of details which would not be within her power if I said I had met a girl in England whom I hoped to make my wife. As to a name, there is no difficulty, because I always referred to you as Bonita, which means pretty, and Spanish people are

45

rather fond of pet names. So, *señorita*, are you reassured? Are you happy to help a man out in a difficulty? There are compensations with regard to the deception, and no one will be hurt by it. Ana is a romantic girl, but she is not in love with me. Madrecita is merely concerned that I settle down to my duties – and you, Lise, will have the holiday of your life before you commence work in Madrid. The job that you so wish for can be arranged without any trouble at all – as I told you, Franquista is a friend of mine.'

Lise noticed how his voice dwelt on the name, and there seemed a sudden aloofness in him as he turned from Lise to rest his hands on the parapet of the veranda and to gaze over his castle and the gardens that rambled to the cliff-like boundary walls.

'Will your brother agree to let you work in Spain?' he asked.

'It isn't for Bob to give me permission,' she half-laughed. 'I am free to do as I wish. Naturally he has always kept a keen eye on me, but he must be shown that I'm now old enough to please myself. I love him very much, and I've always got on well with his wife, but it's time for me to cut free and make a life of my own.'

'And do you think you will like – working in Spain?'

'Yes. It's a warm, vivacious place. The people are so attractive—'

'Really?' he drawled, turning again to look at her, his wide shoulders against the black iron and tawny stone of the parapet. His skin, too, was tawny in the neck-opening of his white shirt, and he had that lean hardness of the man in perfect physical shape. 'It is known in Spain, *señorita*, that the English find us complex but colourful. They see our love of children, and remember our reputation for cruelty. They are astonished that we have so many saints, for they see the devil in our eyes.'

Lise gazed back at him and she felt the sudden quick beating of her heart as she saw the caress and the cruelty in his smile. She knew so little of him and still could not be sure what sort of a man he was, and as she stood there hesitant and unsure, the smile deepened on his lips.

'Don't let it worry you that Spain can cast a spell. The entrancement of a spell holds always an edge of fear. Don't you know that we are the only romantics left in a world of reality?'

'I would hardly call the bullfight a thing of romance,' she argued.

'Perhaps not.' His eyes swept up and down her slender figure. 'It is a duel, and in many respects it holds all the basic elements of what occurs between a man and a woman. The bull is the equivalent of male strength and virility. The cape is the grace and enticement of a woman. The sword, the *espada* himself, is the thrust of sex. But perhaps I should not speak like this to an English girl? There is much talk of the advanced ideas of the English, yet we in Spain still find your people curiously puritan.'

'Spain condemns the bikini,' she scoffed. 'Or so I have heard.'

'Only because it prefers its eroticism to be less crude and more excitingly veiled. There is also the fact that young Spaniards are extremely passionate and it would not do for the nation to have on its hands too many maintenance orders from pretty young tourists. Spain prefers its young men to save themselves for their own girls.'

'Really!' Lise could not suppress a laugh. 'You are arrogant, Señor Conde. And it will appear to everyone that you aren't saving yourself for one of your own girls – though we know between us that you really are, of course.'

His eyes narrowed at her words, until the lashes made dangerous shadows around the glinting irises. 'What do you mean by that remark? What do you think you know of my future plans?'

'I'm not a simpleton, *señor*. I know full well that you are using me to shield another woman . . . the woman you truly wish to marry. You fear your grandmother will disapprove of her—'

'So,' he broke in, 'you are the little witch that you look! You have struck to the root of my dilemma, and now what will you do? Toss back the ring, refuse me this breathing space, and perhaps make it necessary for me to argue with an elderly woman whose heart need not break, one way or the other, unless I have to be brutally honest with her? I think, Miss Harding, that you are too sensitive to risk harming an elderly, charming, if rather autocratic woman.'

'Y-you are not being fair.' Lise couldn't keep a slight stammer of distress out of her voice. 'This entire mix-up is your own fault, not mine. You should have told your grandmother the truth in the first place – she may not care too much that you are in love with a divorced woman—'

And there Lise broke off in horror as he drew in his breath with a slight hiss. She stared at him and fear of how he would react made her grey eyes look enormous.

For several seconds his face was a cold, frightening mask, and then with a shrug almost of irony he allowed it to be admitted that she had guessed his secret.

'She would never forgive me,' he said, in a cold, unemotional voice. 'And I should find it hard to forgive myself if I caused her to have another heart attack. It is natural that I hope she will live for another ten years . . . she is all the real family I have left, but I have been warned that a sudden shock could take her from me. And now, *señorita*, are you satisfied that my dilemma is a very real one? It was, you see, at the time of her heart attack that I invented a fiancée in order to ease her mind, and as you would no doubt remind me, each lie that we tell has its backlash, but the truth in this case would not be possible.'

'I–I see that,' Lise admitted. 'But what if your – oh, you know! What if she should hear of my being here and acting the part of your bogus fiancée? Whatever will she say?'

And then he smiled in the most quizzical way. 'You will know the answer to that question when you are in love yourself. Have you ever seen the opera *Carmen*?'

'Yes, once. Why do you ask?'

'Did it not explain the tragi-comic elements often to be found in Latin love affairs? We can but hope, *señorita*, that neither you nor my Carmen will put a knife into me.'

It was said so casually, and at the same time there was a dark gravity to his eyes that gave away to Lise the unhappiness he felt at not being able to introduce to his grandmother the woman whom he really loved and wanted. However would the situation resolve itself? Did he and Franquista expect to wait years before it was possible for them to marry? Were they lovers already? Lise thought this most likely, and even as the thought filled her mind in all its vivid detail, she found she was clenching her hands behind her and digging that sapphire to the point of pain into her right palm. It was suddenly as if she were feeling a knife in her heart.

'When,' she murmured, 'shall I be expected to meet the Condesa?'

'Later today.' His dark eyes were fixed upon the paleness of Lise's face. 'She keeps to her apartment during the mornings, and sometimes she appears for lunch. But it is usually after four o'clock that she feels fit enough, and sociable enough, to meet people. You look pale and afraid, and that is foolish. She is not a dragon, unless you are judging her by her grandson?'

Lise smiled faintly. 'What will she think of me?'

'That you are young, charming, and with a certain shyness to you.'

'What if she wishes to see me – alone?'

'Don't worry.' He spoke decisively, and stood very tall and regally against the parapet, with the turrets and towers of the *castillo* rising above his dark head. 'There will be no question of that. I shall be with you and any awkward questions will be smoothed over by me. Are you reassured, Lise?'

Once again he mispronounced her name, but she didn't correct him.

'I – I wonder, *señor*, if I could take a walk in your garden? I'm restless and I need the exercise.'

'Of course,' he said. 'There is just one more thing; it would be better if you could bring yourself to call me Leandro. Madrecita will expect a few indications of a – loving relationship between us.'

Her heart seemed to turn right over when he said that, and she had a sudden tormenting vision of all that she had let herself in for. 'Not – not kissing demonstrations, I hope?'

'Who can tell?' He shrugged in a very Latin way, and the quirking of a black eyebrow gave him a devilish look. 'From this moment on we are partners in a game neither of us has played before, and who can tell at this stage what gambits we shall be called upon to make?'

Lise bit her lip, and at once he came across to her and taking hold of her hands he unlocked them and held them. 'Whatever happens,' he drawled, 'the game will never go as far as marriage.'

CHAPTER THREE

IT was a water walk, with the sun-shot arch of water glittering against the green cypresses, the cascades of bougainvillea, and blossom trees scented like citrus and spice.

He walked beside her, the man she had now accepted as her supposed *novio*, very supple and upright, the sun gleaming on the boots that reached to his knees. He pointed out the various flowers and plants to her and she couldn't help but feel a pang of delight at the wild and wonderful array, and at the thousand scents that seemed to go to her head and intoxicate her senses.

Her eyes shone; she was moved by the beauty of it all. Never in her life before had she seen honeysuckle climbing the branches of cypress trees, carnations of every imaginable hue, sheets of violets spreading down banks to the sparkle of a watercourse which fed the garden. Oh, it was much more than a garden! It rambled like a small park, where for years and years each succeeding mistress had added her own choice of plants, until they mingled and married and created a sheer vision of colour and enchantment.

The Conde came to a halt on one of the paths and pointed out a particularly intriguing plant to Lise; it was a coloured nettle called *maja mujer* and he warned her never to try and touch it. Appropriately named 'wicked woman', it would burn the hand and leave a sting.

'An ancestress of mine came from Brazil,' he said, 'and she brought the nettle with her. She was said to resemble it, being vivid and lovely to look at, but with a temper which poured like scalding water from her tongue. You see, not all the brides of the Marcos Reyes have been as gentle as my

51

own mother. Perhaps in some ways she was too gentle.'

'Do you take after your grandmother?' Lise asked dryly.

At once his eyes flashed down at her. She looked away from him, following the shimmering flight of a butterfly in among a great tangle of rose-red, perfect miniature roses. 'Oh dear!' Her hand flew to her lips. 'I hope it won't tear itself on the thorns.'

'I am afraid that is what sometimes happens in the garden of El Serafin,' he said, a note of meaning in his voice. 'A garden is like life itself, with thorns to tear, nettles to sting, stones to make a foot stumble just as one looks up at the sky and sees how blue it is. We each have to be mauled, some time or other, by the tiger of life.'

They left behind them the hedge of roses and came to a small patio set deep within the heart of the garden, its paving tiles glinting under the sun, with stone benches hot from the sun, and there at the centre of it not the usual fountain but a statue of the four seasons, the four female heads each looking in a different direction. One of the strange stone faces seemed to stare at Lise, and as she looked a spider crawled from the partly open lips and involuntarily she drew back and found herself bodily close to the Conde. She felt his hands close on her shoulders and the tremor that ran through her was not entirely caused by the dark, long-legged spider.

'You don't like this place?' He spoke above her head, holding her motionless with her shoulders against his chest. She could feel the hard strength of his body, and the warmth of his fingers, and as she looked about her she was glad that she had not come upon this patio on her own. It had an atmosphere of mystery, somehow, as if something lingered here. Some memory of despair, which only the four stone faces had witnessed.

'I thought you might be sensitive to atmosphere,' he went on. 'It was here that my Brazilian ancestress came to poison herself when her husband learned that she had been having an affair with his brother. In Spain in those days the chastity of a woman was of great importance to a man. His wife had to be an angel of purity and any man who found himself with an unfaithful wife was not condemned by law if he took her life. But Laurita was too proud, too passionate and wilful to submit to punishment and possible death at the hands of her husband, and so she came here and died alone in the dusk of a summer's night. She left a heritage of temper in the Marcos Reyes, and a rebellion against the arranged marriage. Perhaps, *señorita*, I take after her.'

Even as he spoke Lise, without looking at him, could imagine the twist of irony to his lips and the bronze chiselling of the face that held an element of a land even hotter, even more ruthless in its history than Spain itself.

'Laurita was reputed to be the descendant of an Inca princess and a *conquistador*, and I have in the castle a picture of her painted only a short while before she took her own life with all the barbaric courage of her race. Her skin was smooth as porcelain, there were deep blue lights in her hair, and long lashes curled away from her almond-shaped eyes. Her long hair was arranged in shining loops and plaitings, so that her slender neck seemed as if it might break under the weight. She was beautiful, but because she never found real happiness she became bitter, and I believe she turned to another man out of a need for consolation rather than anything else. It is the *anoranza* of Laurita which lingers here. The longing for what she lost, the girlish dream of romance which never materialized because she was handed over to a man she had no time to know before it was time to become his wife. She became in all senses a *maja mujer*, a wicked woman, but I believe she was driven to it by her marriage.

How often must a dowry bride have rebelled in Spain? Often but a girl given to a man quite a few years older than herself; taken straight from convent or schoolroom, never courted by young men of her own age, but expected to be a devoted and loving wife to a stranger. I can imagine that Laurita came often to sit in this patio, but my own mother avoided it. La Soledad, she came to be called. So you see, *señorita*, the adventure of marriage has not been a very happy one for members of my family, and that is why I will not permit yet another young girl to become a bride unloved.'

As he spoke these words he swung Lise to face him. 'Do we now understand each other a little better, eh? Do you see why our meeting had to be put to advantage by me? I could not let you go, to be lost somewhere in Spain, when you had so much the look of this *novia* I had invented for my own sake, for Ana's sake, and the son I might have in the future. I don't wish him to have a mother with such sad eyes that she becomes known as the sad one. Perhaps were we in England such a situation as this would not arise, but we are in Spain, where the pride and the emotions run high. And have I not already said that in exchange for your co-operation I shall give you whatever you wish for most. A new car – a whole new wardrobe of clothes—'

There he paused and his eyes narrowed as he studied Lise. 'I seem always to be seeing you in trousers. Have you no dresses you can wear? Madrecita is old-fashioned and likes girls to look girlish.'

Lise flushed slightly at his criticism. 'I was on a driving holiday and suiting myself, *señor*. I am sorry if you consider I look like a boy, but trousers are comfortable for driving in.'

'Comforting, perhaps, but not so attractive as a display of the female legs. It is one great advantage of the female

54

species that she has beautiful limbs and such a pity that she feels the urge to cover them up as a man does his own. However, we can remedy this lack of feminine apparel, and if you will come with me I shall administer a remedy which should make your eyes shine – always supposing that you are more of a girl than a boy!'

He hurried her back through the garden, around a projection of the castle, in under an archway and up a flight of twisting iron stairs set in one of the towers.

'Where are we going?' she gasped, as if she were being dragged off to Bluebeard's chamber. She heard him give a deep laugh, as if her image of him as Bluebeard transmitted itself to his mind.

'Wait and see and don't anticipate that I am about to ravish you in a lonely tower room of the castle. It is proof of your innocence that you should have such childish thoughts.'

'Not too much a child that I don't suit your purpose,' she gasped, for the stairs were twisting and turning in an endless spiral, and he had longer legs than hers and more lung power. 'Y-you found me handy and naïve enough to help you play a game of make-believe!'

'Games are fascinating, are they not? That is how we must think of what is between us, and in that way we might find it amusing enough to banish the guilt. Let us try, anyway.' And so saying he brought her to a halt on a landing of the tower, with the shield glass of a leaded window showering its colours in a rainbow on his sardonic face, so that instantly he became Harlequin, lord of dangerous games.

A long, arching door confronted them, with a ringed handle, and giving it a turn he opened the door. Lise had somehow expected the room to be unfurnished, but to her amazement it was filled with things. Tall old chairs, chests of drawers, piles of hatboxes, cane hampers, trunks made of leather and looking rather like coffins, and several suits of armour that leered vacantly at Lise as she stood amazed in the doorway of the room.

'A castle has no attic,' said the Conde, looking sardonic and sweeping an arm round the room whose circular walls were timber, and whose windows were lanced with more of that mysterious shield glass that patterned the place with Harlequin colour. 'But a lumber room has to be found for those things that each family likes to hoard. Come!' He pulled Lise across the room towards one of the coffin-like trunks. 'You said you were a needlewoman – very well, *señorita*, see what you can make of this.'

He flung open the lid of the trunk, plunged his hands into it and lifted out for her inspection the most gorgeous array of silks, brocades and velvets Lise had ever seen. She worked for a fashion house and was accustomed to handling rich material, but when she touched the length of jade silk that hung from the Conde's lean hands, she felt within her a hungry longing to fashion and shape it, and feel it softly clinging against her skin. The sort of material she loved, but which as a working girl she could never afford to buy.

'These are sample lengths from our factory,' he explained. 'Whenever my production manager comes to El Serafin he brings these to show Madrecita, who remains interested in the business. Ana will sometimes have a length made into a dress, but she is a raven-haired Latin girl who favours the carmine colours, and so the other jewel colours are abandoned to this old trunk, to lie forgotten. But you are a blonde, *señorita*, and you have grey eyes which can reflect colour rather than clash with it.' He transferred the materials to her arms. 'Here you are! The companion of my grandmother, the Doña Manuela, will be happy to lend you her sewing machine and to assist you in the measuring and cutting of the dresses, and then you will have no excuse for

56

appearing at *merienda* and the late meal, both of which Madrecita attends, clad in a pair of trousers.'

Lise was too astonished by his gift of the fabulous materials to take him up on his remark. She cradled the silk, lace and velvet against her and there rushed through her mind all the designs she could create from these luscious fabrics, and she felt as intoxicated as if he had plied her with Spanish wine.

'How could Ana resist these?' she murmured, and she lifted a fold of the jade silk to her cheek and her grey eyes shone with delight.

'Ana is still very young, sweet but not very subtle,' he replied, and he studied Lise with narrowed eyes as she stroked her cheek with the silk. 'I can see that they appeal to you.'

'They're wonderful, and I don't know how to thank you.'

'I feel sure that you do,' he said, meaningly.

'Oh?' Her eyes widened in contrast to the glinting narrowness of his regard. 'I – I don't understand you. Are there strings attached to the materials?'

'You understand me perfectly well,' he said curtly. 'I wish my grandmother to have no doubts about our so-called alliance, and my gratitude will not stop at a few fabrics if you – play your part well.'

'You—' Lise flushed and bit her lip, 'you make me sound mercenary, as if I'm only interested in what I can get out of you in a material sense. It isn't really like that, and you know it, *señor*. Having spent last night under your roof I am involved whether I like it or not, for I'm sure the rumour has already reached the Condesa that you have brought home with you a – fiancée.'

And as if to support Lise's claim a manservant suddenly appeared in the doorway of the lumber room and she understood some of the Spanish which he addressed to the Conde. The Condesa was asking to speak with him . . . in fact she had sent an order that he was to be brought to her apartment at once! The manservant's eyes flicked to Lise and she guessed what lay behind the Condesa's order, and when Leandro looked at her, she drew back in quick alarm at meeting his grandmother so soon. He frowned slightly, and then told the manservant that he would be along without delay.

When he was alone again with Lise, he gave her a quizzical look. 'You have no need to look so afraid,' he said. 'But all the same I will give you time in which to get used to the idea of meeting the Condesa as her granddaughter-in-law. Come, I will escort you to your own apartment, where you may set about the design of your dresses and try to compose your mind.'

In her present state of confusion she would not have found her way to her suite without a good deal of searching, for though the castle appeared toy-like on the outside, seen against the towering cliffs, it was far from small inside. At last they arrived at her door and he opened it for her. As she moved past him to enter the suite she brushed against his hard frame and again her eyes lifted to his face in an alarm she could not conceal. This was all too real! He was an actual person and not a dream figure, and each time she had contact with him she was made intensely aware of his actuality.

'*Gran cielo!*' The exclamation moved like a whiplash across her pale face. 'You will learn to control that look you have just given me when we are together in Madrecita's company. She has sharp eyes and her wits are in no way impaired by her years. I don't ask you to look faint with love, but on the other hand it won't do for you to look faint with fear. If we are found out in our deception the Condesa won't order the bastinado for you. There are *conqistadors* in our family history, but no inquisitors!'

With these words, and an ironic bow, he turned on his heel and strode off, swiftly turning a bend in the passage so that his tall, breeched and booted figure was out of Lise's sight ... but not out of her memory. His every feature seemed stamped upon her mind, and his every intonation rang there. She closed her door, but his looks and his words entered with her, and she hastened to the bed and dropped the luscious fabrics down upon it, as if all at once they burned her. They lay in a softly glistening heap, and she knew that in a while her delight in them would reassert itself, but right now she had to remove herself to the veranda where she sank down into the cane easy chair and felt as if each nerve in her body was stretched taut and must relax before she screamed, or threw a vase in order to relieve her feelings.

What had she got herself into?

This time yesterday she had been a free and happy tourist, and the little red car had not shown a sign of going wrong on a lonely mountain road.

She sighed and stretched out her legs in the trousers *he* disapproved of. He was giving her orders as if their engagement was real instead of bogus, and she had to accept them, or make a dash for freedom while he was with his grandmother and deep in conversation with her. Lise half rose, then sank back in her chair, allowing her head to rest in a sort of defeat against the wide fan back of the chair.

It was no use ... she was honour bound to keep the bargain she had made with him. He would now be telling his grandmother about her ... the Condesa de Marcos Reyes, who would soon be eighty years of age, and whose heart was not strong enough to stand up to a sudden shock ... such as being told that her grandson's *novia* had run away from the castle. Having had her hopes built up, the Condesa would then have them shattered again, and Lise could not face the responsibilty of what that might do to a proud and elderly woman who probably only lived now to see the wedding of her grandson.

The presentation of a *novia* would at least promise this, and Lise was too soft-hearted to shatter that promise.

She closed her eyes against the down-beating sun and felt the golden warmth against her face and her neck. Whatever happened not a word of all this must reach her brother. Both he and his wife had been opposed to this trip she had insisted on making alone, and all of this would strike their very logical and down-to-earth minds as sheer lunacy.

Her lips moved in a slight smile, but now she could feel some of the tension easing out of her body, and she supposed it was because she had finally accepted the fact that she was committed to play the part of bride-to-be of a handsome, worldly Spaniard, who was not only rich but who was titled, and whose home was a tawny-stoned castle.

If it were all true, and would end for her in wedding bells and real love, she would at this moment have been feeling rather like Cinderella to whom the silver slipper had been fitted with success. Bird calls echoed from the trees around the castle, and they seemed to hold a mocking note. They seemed to keep reminding her that it was all makebelieve and not for a moment must she lose sight of the fact that the beauty of the castle was hers to enjoy for only a few days, maybe a week and no more.

A vision returned to her of all the vivid, riotous flowers and plants she had been shown during her walk through the gardens with Leandro ... ah, already she was beginning to think of him by name, but she couldn't face, as yet, the thought of addressing him in that way. With an Englishman it was an informality ... but with a Spaniard it seemed strangely intimate. It was as if something in the Spanish atmosphere created a deeper awareness of men as men, and women as women. That air of good companionship so prevalent in England was absent from the man-woman relationship in Spain. It was as if a touch of the pagan still lingered here, to remind women that men still had the strength to overpower them, and so they must be charming in order to control their strong and sensual men.

Lise felt her hands gripping the arms of her chair and she realized now she was alone how many things she had noticed about Leandro de Marcos Reyes during their walk together. The way his raven-dark hair sprang back from his brow, and how the muscles had rippled in his forearm when he had raised a hand to fondle the fruit of a tree. In the neck-opening of his shirt the chain of a religious medal had glinted, a lighter gold against the tawny gold of his skin. And when he had rested a booted foot upon a low stone wall, there had been more than a hint of the tamer about him.

She wondered what were his secret thoughts when he compared a naïve English girl like herself to the vivid, worldly woman whom Lise had met in England without ever dreaming that she would also meet the man who had not denied loving Franquista.

He must be secretly amused by the comparison, for the Spanish woman had dressed with perfection, and her dark smooth hair had been a perfect frame for her camellia-skinned face, in which her eyes had sparkled like enormous dark gems. Whatever the bitterness lingering from her broken marriage it hadn't showed ... but no wonder Leandro was opposed to the arranged marriage! It had not only hurt his mother and made her unhappy. It had also made difficult his future with Franquista. Even if he kept from his grandmother the fact of Franquista's divorce, she would be bound to learn of it from someone else and be shockingly opposed to the match. Being of the old régime she would not recognize divorce and it would seem to her that her beloved grandson was living in sin. The shock might even kill her.

His dilemma was acute, but Lise didn't doubt that he meant to marry Franquista, and that was why he was ensuring that the Condesa did not involve him with her ward Anastasia.

Lise, as the girl at the centre of the drama, wasn't sure how she felt about it all. One half of her fervently wished for escape from the *castillo*, while the more adventurous half wished to stay and see what happened . . . as if it were a play! She went back into her bedroom and tidied the dress fabrics, running her fingers over the silky surface of them and trying not to imagine Audrey's scandalized face, did she know that her young sister-in-law had become this involved with a man in less than twenty-four hours. When Audrey talked about her 'settling down' she meant with some nice, reasonably ambitious, and far from unpredictable young man.

Lise was quite certain that Audrey would consider Leandro de Marcos Reyes the very opposite to her ideal 'young man'. And she would be appalled that Lise, who had been so carefully brought up, so guarded and cared for by Bob, should allow herself to be talked into a bogus engagement by a man, and all because he was the very epitome of the dark and dangerously handsome Latin.

As she folded the materials Lise told herself that she was in no way influenced by his looks, his self-assurance, and his quick ability to grasp what was advantageous to him. He was ruthless, and never in her life before had Lise met a truly ruthless man, who took what he wanted as his *conquistador* ancestors had done.

Though she denied to herself that she found him exciting,

her mind mocked her for a little liar.

It was about eleven o'clock when Lise decided to return to the courtyard to see if there was any tea to be had. To her delight she was in time to see a maid carrying a tray to a white, lacy iron table set beneath the shade of a camellia tree, and at the table sat a young, sedate figure with a book in her hands.

Lise approached the girl and said good morning. The girl glanced up, revealing a round and pretty face framed in silky dark hair. Her eyes were large, honey-coloured, and rather shy. She returned Lise's greeting, and with reserve in her voice she added: 'I am pleased to meet the English *novia* of the Señor Conde. We have all been wondering about you and could not tell what you would really be like because Leandro would not describe you in detail. I hope very much that you will like being here at El Serafin. This is the nicest time of the year, when the sun is hot but not burning. I – I would be pleased if you would join me for tea and cakes. I cannot resist cream cakes, though Madrina warns me that I shall be as plump as Florentina.'

Lise smiled and sat down in one of the white chairs that matched the table. 'I know you are Ana. I was told by – by Leandro how pretty you are, and quite truthfully I only wish I could put on a little more weight and not be quite so meagre.'

'You are very slender,' Ana said, with a little sigh of envy. But when the plate of delicious-looking cakes was placed on the table, she broke into a smile and gazed at them with youthfully greedy eyes. 'It is no use, if I get as big as a house I cannot resist Florentina's cakes. You must taste one, or perhaps two.'

'I shall be delighted.' Lise helped herself to a slice of cream and nut pastry, but it was a cup of tea for which she was thirsting, and as soon as it was poured she was drinking it. The sun through the loaded boughs of creamy-white flowers glinted on the silver teapot, and found tiny blue lights in Ana's hair. Looking at the girl, taking note of her neat prettiness in a white dress spattered with bunches of pale mauve flowers, Lise could understand both the Condesa's wish to have her betrothed to Leandro, and his wish not to hurt the girl in any way that would be lasting.

Anastasia was nice, but far too dove-natured for the liking of a hawk such as Leandro. She would never be a challenge for him; never brave enough to oppose him in any way. Always she would submit without question, and be honey when he needed fire.

It was then, as she drank tea with Ana beneath the camellia tree, that Lise accepted her invidious position as his supposed bride-to-be. She relaxed in her seat and lifted her face to the dappling of sun and shadow. 'I hoped,' she said. 'I hoped very much that we could be friends.'

'But you were afraid I would hate you,' said Ana, 'because you are the one chosen by Leandro. You must be feeling very, very happy.'

'I'm ecstatic,' Lise smiled, indulging her sense of humour and yet aware at the same time that Ana would take her seriously. 'These are very tasty cakes – and, please, may I have another cup of tea? All this sun makes me feel rather thirsty.'

'You think you will like living in Spain?' Ana asked.

This was one question which Lise could answer truthfully, for she still planned to stay in Spain if Franquista's offer of employment still remained open. 'I think I'm going to love your country,' she said. 'It has a golden quality ... here at least, if not so much in the cities. I understand from Leandro that you have lived at El Serafin for several years. How lovely to live in a castle!'

'You, also, will be living in the castle.' Ana helped herself to another pastry and she looked at Lise from under her long silky lashes. 'Will you mind that I am here? You see, I have nowhere else to go and I am so fond of Madrina. She has been so good to me, and so has Leandro – almost like a brother.'

'I am delighted that you are here,' Lise said quickly, with the fervent warmth of someone who felt she was going to need a friend. 'I hope we can be real companions, and that you will show me all the local beauty spots and places of interest.'

'But you will have Leandro to do all that,' Ana widened her eyes at Lise, as if detecting in her voice a small note of desperation. 'The *castillo* is his pride and joy, and there is much land planted with all sorts of trees and flowers, which he was once requested to allow the *turistas* to see, but he refused and said that El Serafin was private family property and he asked if the tourists would like their own gardens trampled all over.' A smile shimmered in Ana's eyes. 'He is afraid of no one – except perhaps he is afraid of hurting Madrina.'

'I can understand his objection to having his gardens thrown open to a lot of strangers, and I can understand his concern for the Condesa. He has his human side,' Lise added, with a small, rather choked laugh.

'But of course,' said Ana. 'You must know of that side to him, being the girl he has chosen to be his partner in life. It is a very important role to play, and many girls have hoped—' Ana broke off and pretended that a gay and sparkling hummingbird, no larger than a large butterfly, had taken her interest. 'See how it whirls round and round the hibiscus flowers. They have a deep scented heart which is said to drive the hummingbird to distraction. It is like a jewel, no?'

'It's gorgeous,' Lise agreed gently, for she had just been

shown a glimpse of Ana's heart. The girl had hoped that Leandro would come to love her, and now she had to accept with grace that he only wished to be a sort of brother, kindly disposed but not romantically drawn to her pretty face and her gentleness. Like the gaily winged hummingbird he was attracted to what was vivid and perfumed.

Lise could not tell Ana the truth, so she changed the subject and asked if they were close to a beach. 'Where cliffs abound there is usually some ocean to be held back,' she said gaily. 'I rather like to swim, but I'm not very fond of crowded beaches. I'm greedy and like the sands and the sea almost to myself. I don't mind a friend or two, and a few crabs.'

'We are above the sea, but it is a long way down to the beach. I am not fond of the water.' Ana gave a little shiver. 'The waves throw you about and the salt takes all the shine out of your hair. But I do know that the English like the sea. When we heard that Leandro had become affianced to an *inglesa* I asked Chano Velarde to tell me about the English, as he had been there himself on business for the factory, and he told me how fair-skinned were the girls, and how they liked to wear very short skirts and loved getting wet in the water. At first I could not imagine Leandro in love with a girl such as this, but now we have met I can see why he admires you. Your hair is so bright, and your eyes are beautiful, and you seem not to be afraid of anything.'

'I try not to be,' Lise flushed a little at the compliment paid to her eyes. In England people weren't given to flattery, and it had never occurred to her to consider herself anything more than fairly presentable. Now it came as a bit of a shock to realize that Leandro de Marcos Reyes would not have considered her a suitably convincing *novia* if she had been plain and dowdy. She recalled how he had stared at her in the light of his headlamps last night, and once he had found

66

out that she was travelling alone he had lost no time in entangling her in his web of deception Her flush deepened. and she sought to escape from the thought of him.

'Who is Chano Velarde?' she asked, reaching up casually to cup a camellia in the palm of her hand. To think they grew like this in a Spanish garden, and were so expensive to buy in England, where they had to be grown under glass.

'Chano works for the Señor Conde and upon occasion he comes here to the *castillo*.' A note of vivacity had crept into Ana's voice, and directly Lise heard it she recalled what Leandro had said about a certain friend of his and the regard he had for Ana. The intimation had been that this friend would welcome the news that Ana was free to be approached by another man with an affectionate regard for her.

'Is he nice?' Lise smiled at the other girl. 'I like his name.'

'He is not so tall as Leandro, or so – so commanding, but he is very good-looking.' A flush stole under the soft and creamy skin of the Condesa's ward, who had probably kept her feelings for Chano under lock and key in case it was arranged that she marry the Conde. Now those feelings could be released, and Lise had a sudden happy sense of something good coming of this false engagement. But she mustn't dwell on that! Her fingers tightened on the petals of the camellia and all at once they showered down on to her hair. As she brushed at them Ana gave a laugh.

'That is an omen that you will be married soon,' she said.

'Oh no.' The words were out before Lise could prevent them. 'I mean, a couple can't rush into marriage so soon after the – the engagement. They must become more accustomed to each other—'

'But you have been the *novia* of Leandro for a year,' Ana protested. 'The Condesa will not permit her grandson to

67

wait very much longer before the wedding. She will insist – is probably insisting right this moment that he set the arrangements in motion.'

'He – he can't do that!' In a sudden panic Lise almost jumped to her feet and made a dash for the castle gates and freedom. What held her back was the sudden approach of a tall figure through the trees, clad right now in a light grey lounge suit which intensified his dark and striking Spanish looks. Lise was looking directly at him, and the panic was plain to see in her eyes. His eyes narrowed and his black brows contracted, but when he reached the table there was a nonchalant air about him and he made no comment on the sudden look of fright on Lise's face.

'You are making friends, no?' He seated himself on a waist-high wall nearby, which guarded the orange and lemon trees, the fruits hanging there in the sunlight like coloured globes. He directed a smile from Ana to Lise, and she thought how superbly sure of himself he looked and wished she might catch a little of that assurance and not feel that at any moment she was going to give herself away as a fraud. She had almost done so a moment ago, when Ana had said that his grandmother would expect his wedding plans to be put into activity as soon as possible.

'I hope your grandmother is feeling well,' she said to him.

'She is feeling wonderful,' he said with satisfaction. 'She desires to meet you at *merienda* this afternoon, when we will open a bottle of champagne and celebrate.'

Lise met his suave smile and she wished they were alone so she could insist that he didn't involve her in bogus wedding plans as well as a bogus engagement. 'I didn't know that Spanish people drank champagne,' she said. 'I thought you preferred your own wines.'

'We do, as a rule,' he agreed. 'But there are occasions

when the gold wine is appropriate, and Madrecita will expect it. She is looking forward to meeting you and I had better warn you in advance that she plans to give you a present.'

'But—'

He held up a restraining hand, and he shot a quizzical smile at Ana. 'The British are very independent, Ana. You would not believe the trouble I had to persuade this girl to become engaged to me. She had the mistaken idea that she would not be popular with my family. Was that not an absurd notion? She thought she would be found strange and unlike us – a white rose among the red.'

Ana smiled back at him, and Lise saw the shyness in her eyes. She supposed that most women, even those who knew him fairly well, would always find him rather intimidating, rather lordly, the natural Latin pride intensified in someone who was the titled master of a castle and the land that stretched to the *sierras* and the sea.

'Lise is very pretty,' said Ana. 'We all expected that she would be from the diminutive which you gave her when you first told us that you had met her in England. She is very *bonita.*'

'There you are,' he said to Lise, a softly mocking note in his voice. 'I told you that you had nothing to fear from Ana or the Condesa. They are only too delighted that you are to be related to them.'

'Well,' she gave a forced laugh, 'nothing is settled for sure, is it, *señor*? You and I mightn't find ourselves compatible on Spanish soil together. In the event of this we should not go as far as – marriage, should we? I mean, marriage is such a commitment in the eyes of Spanish people, and I hope you explained to the Condesa that we are not making any definite arrangements until – well, until we are sure of our – feelings.'

'The British are also rather cautious,' he informed Ana, a quirk to his eyebrow. 'Even when they fall in love at first sight they are inclined to tell themselves – at first – that they have a slight case of fever and the dizziness will soon wear off. Their women are so intriguing, for they are ice-maidens with souls of fire, and a man can never be sure when that coolness will become a passionate glow.'

This was said in such a nonchalant fashion that Lise decided not to take him seriously . . . until she caught his gaze upon her and saw how his eyes were glinting, as if his own words had taken on a sudden significance and could be put to the test. Her own gaze jerked away from his and fell to his lips . . . firmly bold lips, and yet with that disturbing hint of strong Latin passions.

Lise tried to thrust away from her the image of those lips on hers, warm and curved . . . demanding and a tiny bit cruel. She tried not to see his shoulders and how they would blot out the world when he bent over a woman She tried – angrily – not to imagine how warm and gold his skin would be to the touch of her hand.

Because she so wildly resented her own thoughts she looked at him with resentment. 'I – I don't wish anything definite to be arranged,' she said. 'We – must make sure of our feelings. After all, we have known each other such a short time.'

'A year is a short time?' Ana queried, looking from Leandro to Lise with amazed eyes.

'Lise means that we have not spent a year together,' he broke in smoothly. 'Come, *amada*, don't look so uneasy. I have not made plans to shut you in my Spanish tower.'

Although he smiled, quirking his eyebrow in that faintly mocking way of his, Lise did not smile with him. The more she saw of him, the more convinced she became that he would never really consider her feelings if this false betrothal got out of hand. It was the Condesa who must not be hurt . . . Lise Harding was young and resilient and could be expected to recover from whatever traumas she encountered here at El Serafin – even the trauma of finding her emotions stirred up and shaken for the first time in her life!

The look he gave Lise, passing his eyes over the dappled gold of her hair and the cool blue of her shirt, told her that he meant to have his way and could manage easily the rebellions of a mere girl.

'I hope you have at least one dress you can wear this afternoon,' he said. 'Otherwise Ana can lend you one of hers. Madrecita is old-fashioned and she associates trousers with the male sex, and as we know there is a fashion among young English boys at present for wearing the hair on the shoulders. I wish you to make an attractive impression, *novia mia*, if you will be so good.'

'I take it you are giving me an order?' she rejoined.

'If you like, *pequeño*.' His gaze was so direct that it was almost a touch; his voice was so silky it was menacing.

'What if I don't like?' She tossed her chin, as if inviting him to cuff it.

'Do you really wish me to answer that question?' he drawled.

'It seems that my wishes are going to be disregarded anyway,' she said. 'But to set your mind at ease, *señor*, I do have a dress I can wear and I wouldn't dream of upsetting the Condesa by defying the conventions she lives by. I am sure she is a remarkable person and I am looking forward to meeting her.'

'You understand that she will wish to explore your personality.' His eyes narrowed, holding Lise's gaze like magnets. 'She will be most curious about you, and will wish to probe in order to find the substance of you. I hope you will stand up to her.'

'I shall certainly do my best,' Lise said spiritedly. At once the sardonic smile line deepened in his cheek, and she swore to herself then and there to treat the whole thing in a carefree manner and to dismiss from her mind the vaguest suspicion that he would embroil her any deeper. After all, she knew about Franquista, and he was most unlikely to allow the Condesa to make any arrangements that might upset his real plans for the future.

Having faced this small Armageddon, the day took on a gayer aspect for Lise, and she returned his mocking smile with a perky smile of her own.

'I am sure Ana has decided that we are a terribly quarrelsome pair, who will never make it to the altar anyway,' she said.

'*Amada*,' he drawled, extracting from the endearment a sort of relish, as if he well knew how much she disliked being his sham darling. 'Ana is well aware of the Latin liking for these verbal duels and she would be astounded if I did not indulge in them with my bride-to-be. What is a meal worth if it has no salt and pepper to give it flavour?'

'And what is a meal without a little sweet?' she flashed back at him.

'Ah, if it is a little sweet you are requiring, then I shall be only too happy to provide it.' He rose to his feet with a lithe movement of his lean and supple body and a single stride had brought him to the side of the table where Lise sat. He was bending as if to plant a kiss on her cheek when a sudden pattering of feet brought a flurried little lady into the courtyard, all rustling bombazine and waving hands and the gleam of tortoiseshell combs in a mass of grey hair piled above an anxious face.

'Señor Conde, you must come at once to the Condesa!

She has decided that she wishes right now to meet your *novia* and she is working herself into a state.'

'But she was perfectly all right when I left her half an hour ago.' He stood there, tall and dark, frowning at the agitated companion. 'She was about to read a few letters and she appeared quite pleased and composed.'

'I believe, *señor*,' an agitated glance was flung at Lise, 'I have a feeling it was something she read in one of her letters that brought on this insistence that she see you again, accompanied by the young lady.'

Still with brows drawn he fingered his chin. 'Very well, Manuela. The Señorita Harding and myself will come to speak with Madrecita. H'm, so she became discomposed after reading a letter ... was it one of those she received from Madrid, by any chance?'

'I believe so, Señor Conde. The contents seemed very much to upset her, and that was when she became insistent that I bring you to her room again, but not alone this time. I hope, *señor*, that you were not about to go anywhere? I don't like to disturb you, but—'

'I understand perfectly, Manuela.' He smiled down at the anxious little woman. 'Please not to look so distracted, and return calmly to tell the Condesa that we are on our way to see her.'

'You are good, *señor*.' The companion bustled away, a chain of beads clinking against the jet buttons fastening the bodice of her rather dated dress. Lise gazed after her and decided that she was a nice old thing, obviously devoted to the Condesa, to whom she had probably given the best years of her life. Perhaps she was an impoverished relative, for Lise understood that most Spanish *duennas* were of the poor branch of a family and glad to give their service and companionship in exchange for food and board. It was a way of life as mid-Victorian as Manuel's mode of dress ... and

Lise couldn't help wondering if the Condesa's rules of conduct were equally old-fashioned.

'We had better go to her.' Leandro's shadow loomed over Lise once more, but now the mocking enjoyment was gone from his eyes and they were sombre, and shadowed by his lashes. He took Lise by the arm and drew her upright. 'You will be all right all alone, Ana?' he asked.

'I shall read my book, *señor*,' she replied, and at the same time she shot a look of friendly encouragement at Lise. '*Até a vista.*'

Lise walked towards the castle with Leandro, and still his fingers were locked about her arm ... and when suddenly she felt a strange, electric thrill right through her body from his touch, she said breathlessly:

'Should I go and change into a dress, *señor*?'

'There is no time for that.' He spoke almost curtly. 'She will have to accept you as you are!'

Lise wanted to protest against this, to say that he must allow her to tidy her hair, make up her mouth, and not look as if he were dragging her to the slaughter. But the protesting movement of her arm made his fingers tighten, until she gave a little gasp and knew herself bruised.

CHAPTER FOUR

THE small *salon* of the Condesa's suite was so charming that for a few minutes it diverted Lise's thoughts from her actual meeting with the grandmother of the man who ushered her into the room. There were delightful corner cabinets with china and ornaments on display, a beautiful rose-pink carpet, tapestry furniture, and an immense ancestral painting surrounded by wonderful carvings of eagles and foliage and strange fruits.

Lise couldn't help staring at the portrait, for though she knew from the uniform the man was wearing that he could not be Leandro, the resemblance to the present Conde was startling. There was that same commanding lift to the head, that same dark line of brow above the haughty, handsome features.

'They called him El Conquistadore.' Leandro spoke suddenly above her head, startling her a little, so that she turned to look at him before realizing how the living eyes could shake her nerves far more than the painted ones. 'He went wherever there was glory to be found for Spain, and gold, of course.'

'I have heard that the *conquistadors* were cruel,' she murmured, her fingers stealing to her upper arm, where she knew she would find bruises when she removed her shirt.

'It has always been a Spanish trait in some matters,' he admitted. 'But don't forget, *señorita*, that here in Spain we have no need for an authority to guard against cruelty to children. We love children and respect age and wisdom.'

'Then quite a bit of your cruelty must be directed against women,' she dared to say, her own fingers tightening on his bruises, almost as if for a moment she needed to feel pain.

'Women,' he said, gazing down deliberately into her eyes, 'are strangely enough not averse to a little cruelty . . . if they love the man.'

'That sounds a bit of a paradox,' she argued. 'Or a man's excuse for making use of his extra bit of physical strength. I – I don't think I should enjoy cruelty, even from someone I might love.'

'You speak from only innocent experience,' he said, soft-stroking her with his mockery. 'Love itself is an emotion close to masochism, not only in a physical sense but in a spiritual one. To love truly and with great depth one should be prepared to be martyred for the sake of the loved one. But no doubt your cool British soul shrinks from such an idea? Love for you would be the good companion, not the passionate captor.'

'What is wrong with good, kind companionship?' she asked. 'Better to be warm than always on fire.'

He laughed at her, then, and his laughter was like dark honey, pepper and rocks. 'How little you know,' he mocked, 'how much you have to learn. I almost envy the man who must inevitably come along as your trainer.'

'I notice,' a pert note slipped into her voice, 'that you use the word in preference to teacher. I almost begin to believe, *señor,* that you regard women as wild cats who must be whipped into purring for you, and fawning over you.'

'What an intriguing imagination you have, Lise,' and into his eyes, in that instant, there leapt a tiny flame, a distinct glow, as if she had kindled in him a desire to probe her personality with his keen and worldly mind. The very thought of being probed by him was enough to tighten her nerves. There was no knowing what he might dig up for his delectation; what hidden secret he might uncover for his amusement.

Slim and tensed, she turned again to the vivid portrait. 'Your conquering ancestor wears a magnificent uniform,' she said. 'And you are very like him to look at.'

'I am sure you mean that we resemble each other in ways as well,' he drawled. 'Madrecita always says that she keeps the portrait in her apartment because I refuse to have a self-portrait executed for her; she says further that that is how I truly see myself. Perhaps she is correct, eh? I am certain you would agree with her.'

'I do agree,' Lise admitted. 'Is there not a belief that those alike in body are alike in heart; that every now and again there is a reincarnation of a devil or a saint?'

'*Demonio*,' the word escaped him like the soft hiss of a whip, 'you are tempting me to retaliate. Is that what you want, even though you may not know it? Are you testing me to see how far I will go in taming a woman? I am no saint, admittedly, but I can be a devil when put to the test.'

'You will apply no such test to me!' Lise backed away from him and her fingers tensed as if she would claw him if he dared to touch her. His eyes mocked and gleamed and anything might have happened if at that moment the inner door hadn't opened to admit Manuela into the small *salon*. Lise's sigh of relief blended with the companion's cry of delight that they had arrived to see the Condesa.

Lise touched a hand to her hair and wished to goodness that he had allowed her to go and make herself a little more presentable. One moment he had talked of the unsuitability of the trousers she was wearing, and the next he was saying that she must meet the Condesa clad in them. Lise took a deep breath of air, like a swimmer plunging into unknown depths, and walked with Leandro de Marcos Reyes to the door of his grandmother's bedroom. He gestured to Lise to precede him and she did so, feeling like a little automaton which had been wound up for this moment and would surely

77

break down after it.

She had expected regality and was not disappointed. She stared at the magnificent velvet hangings of the daised bed, with a crown-shaped canopy to hold the gleaming yards of lavender material. She saw the curving line of windows giving on to the romantic, fabled view of the castle turrets. In a great alabaster vase there were peonies of deep, glowing pink. And in the bed itself, looking splendidly arrogant, was a woman who had always been superbly beautiful. As a young woman her hair would have been as raven as Leandro's, but now it was a gleaming silver toque above a pair of demanding dark eyes, made all the more striking by the mascara and shadow which was applied to them. Rouge lay like peony petals over the high cheekbones, and the full lips were painted.

Lise could feel herself staring, for when Leandro had mentioned that his grandmother was old-fashioned, a picture of her in dark Victorian clothes had sprung to mind, with severity written all over a handsome but unpowdered face.

Instead Lise saw a woman clad in a lace bedjacket of deep mauve, huge silk pillows behind her shoulders, the rose-pink silken cover of her huge bed strewn with magazines, letters, combs, mirrors, sweet boxes and jewellery boxes.

It was like walking into the glamorous boudoir of a very great actress ... or an empress, and Lise had the rather hysterical feeling that she ought to curtsy or something.

Instead she watched wide-eyed as Leandro approached the Condesa and stood looking down at her with a quizzical expression on his face. When he spoke he used English words so Lise would understand him with greater ease.

'Here we are, Madrecita, at your command. Manuela informs me that you have an insatiable curiosity to meet my *novia pronto*.' He turned to Lise and beckoned her to the bedside. He stood below the three steps of the dais, tall enough to meet his grandmother's eyes, but Lise saw at once that she would have to mount them, and as she did so, she was acutely aware of the Condesa taking her in from top to toe. At once she felt untidy, at a disadvantage, and a terrible fraud. She could hardly believe that she had allowed herself to get into such a bogus situation, yet here she was, under scrutiny by a proud and alarming member of the Latin aristocracy, who was meant to believe that her equally proud and alarming grandson had chosen for his bride-to-be a girl with tousled fair hair, a face that could never be called anything more than youthfully charming, and a figure that was more sleek than curvaceous.

The Condesa was bound to see through the farce, and even as Lise felt certain that she saw a flicker of derision in the fine, painted eyes, the grandmother of Leandro put out her ringed hands to Lise and said warmly:

'Welcome to El Serafin, my child. Leandro has told me about you, of course, but seeing a man's intended bride in person is different from making an image of her in one's mind.' The fingers glittering with jewels caught at Lise's hands with surprising strength and closed about them with a sort of tenacity. For a panicky moment Lise almost pulled away, and very nearly cried out that she wasn't the figment of the imagination dreamed up by Leandro in order to protect him against the arranged marriage . . . the sort of marriage which had made much of his mother's life unhappy.

Panic almost won, and then was defeated as the Condesa pulled Lise right down to her and with a dominating look in her eyes, said sweetly but firmly: 'You may kiss me, child. You have an interesting young face, and I welcome you as a future member of the Marcos Reyes family, which I am sure you realize is an old and powerful one despite the fact that it has been reduced to one old lady and one virile young man, who I am glad to see is at last facing up to his responsibilities with regard to the continuation of our line.'

So saying the Condesa presented her cheek and Lise placed her lips against the perfumed skin. 'Thank you, *señora*, for your kind welcome,' she said, like a polite child who had been tutored by a firm adult.

'You may call me Madrecita, but tell me, child, do you wear male nether garments all the time? I hope you won't mind if I say that I disapprove of them? If the legs of women had been meant to be concealed, I am sure Mother Nature would not have wasted time giving more shape to them than she has given to masculine legs. I fail to understand the modern girl. In my youth skirts were long and even if one had shapely legs they were not allowed to show above the ankle. Now it is permissible to show the leg, young women prefer to hide it in the garment of the man. The long skirt has a certain mystery, but the trousers worn by women only create an effect of stumpiness. The long skirt can add grace, but trousers – never!'

'I'm sorry,' Lise flushed, and would not have dared to rebel against the Condesa's tirade as she had rebelled with Leandro. He had merely been sarcastically amused by her appearance, but it was very plain that the Condesa had always been an elegant woman herself and she wasn't being unkind for the sake of hurting Lise but for the sake of fashion itself.

'I – I would have changed before coming to see you, but your *duenna* said it was urgent that we come, and – and Leandro said there was no time for primping.' Lise bit her lip as she felt him stir behind her and stand tall beside her on the steps of the dais. And she felt as if every separate nerve in her body had a barb in it has his arm slid around her; it was almost as if the skin of her waist was bare, so acute was his touch.

'Yes, why the urgency, Madrecita?' he asked. 'What caused you to change your mind about meeting Lise later today — when I am sure she would have been looking her most attractive?'

His grandmother studied his face intently, and it seemed to Lise that she was looking for some small sign of guilt; some rift in his suave mask. It was as if she sensed that he was playing a game with her, and she in turn would play a game with him. Lise felt like the innocent pawn between them . . . and was too fascinated by the pair of them to really mind.

For the briefest moment the Condesa hesitated in her reply to him, and then her jewelled fingers gleamed as she gestured at a letter which looked as if it had been thrust with anger into its blue envelope. That it was written on coloured paper indicated that it had been sent by a woman, and Lise watched as a long fingernail stabbed at the letter.

'As you are aware, Leandro, I still have old friends in Madrid, and now that I do not go there quite so much they write to regale me with the latest gossip.' The Condesa glanced from his face to Lise's. 'Now I have actually met this young girl, whom you have spoken about but never produced before, I imagine I can discard the information contained in this letter from Tereseta Delmonde, who, as you know, has an apartment in the centre of Madrid so she can be near the fashion shops and the theatres and restaurants.'

The Condesa paused and fixed her eyes so intently upon the face of her grandson that it was as if she tried to read his mind. 'Do I now understand that your various meetings with that notorious South American woman were for business purposes only? My friend Tereseta has seen you together at the smart restaurants of Madrid, and at the Opera House and the *corrida*. It would be like that creature to enjoy the bullfight, but you know my feelings, Leandro. Despite the fact that I am Latin, I deplore the excessive callousness of the bullring, and I have said many times that any woman who enjoys seeing a man ravished by sharp horns, or a bull barbed and stabbed to death, is a woman who lives for passion and not for love. I say nothing to your affairs, if you must have them, but I hope and pray I can be assured you mean to marry this girl you bring here today. She has innocence even if she lacks seduction, and I warn you—'

'Madrecita,' he held up a warning hand, 'I have told you often enough before that I won't be dictated to. I promised I would bring to you an English girl of unimpeachable character, did I not? Well, here she is, she stands at my side, and is real enough for you to have felt her kiss, and possibly her trembling. She comes of a family who have guarded her well, and if you give her the impression I am a man of affairs, she will thrust back at me the ring she wears for me.'

With that deep laugh of his, in which mockery seemed to have a permanent place, he lifted Lise's left hand and showed it to the Condesa. 'See, she wears the family sapphire. It is on the hand of an innocent girl, so you can relax and forget the gossip of your friend Tereseta. You know as well as I that for business purposes I must meet all kinds of men and women, and if it is entertaining for them to visit the *corrida*, then must I, like a callow boy, say that my grandmother disapproves?'

Abruptly he broke into a smile. 'You are like most beautiful women, Madrecita. You like your own way most of the time, and consider your views of life as impeccable as your own face in a mirror. When you speak of love I wonder if you mistake the word for duty.'

Her eyes flashed when he said this. 'Be in no doubt, Leandro, that you owe duty to your name and your position, but I think I have demonstrated over the years that I have great love for you, and that is why I wish you to have a girl for your wife who will continue with the love after I am gone. You are much of a man, Leandro. Easy for a woman to look at and desire, but not so easy for a woman to live with you in harmony – unless she has a warm, receptive, tolerant nature. I admit now that your mother was the wrong choice for your father, that she had a withdrawn nature, to be cloistered rather than exposed to the natural demands of a strong and virile man. But that does not mean that you must go to the opposite extreme in order to find your married happiness, and I am glad that you have seen wisdom and placed your ring upon the hand of this English girl. Naturally enough I had hopes that you would turn to – well, to a young Latin girl, but this one is *bonita*, as you said, and she will do better than that *other*.' There was such sudden venom in the Condesa's voice, such a flash of indignation in her eyes, that Lise could understand fully Leandro's unhappy dilemma in loving and wanting this victim of his grandmother's actue displeasure. How could he bring Franquista here? How could he admit that 'the notorious South American woman' was the woman he desired to marry? Unable to stay away from Franquista in Madrid, the fact of their meetings had already found their way to the Condesa, and now it occurred to Lise that she must have appeared to him, on that lonely road in a broken-down car, like a blessing dropped into his hands out of the blue.

Now he was holding very tightly to her hand, and the blue fire of his ring was burning against the whiteness of her skin, catching and holding the Condesa's gaze.

'It is the custom for a *novia* to give to the *novio* a ring in exchange for his, to seal the bond. Has Leandro told you, child?'

Lise shook her head, and added with an attempt at

humour: 'I'm afraid I have very little to give him in exchange, not even a dowry or a hope chest. My kind of work doesn't pay high wages, you see, and I just about saved enough to come here.'

Lise spoke the words in all innocence, and it wasn't until she saw the sharpening of the Condesa's eyes, and heard the quick intake of breath at her side, that she fully realized the slip she had made. Then Leandro spoke into the small breach of silence. 'You see how British and independent is my *novia*, Madrecita. All she has so far agreed to accept from me is the betrothal ring, and some silks so she can indulge her passion for designing and making dresses. It is very difficult for such a girl to allow herself to be fussed over and spoiled and she cannot comprehend our custom of making much of a future bride. In her country marriage has become a partnership rather than a bonding of two separate lives into one heart, one soul. As you can imagine, I have much to teach her, and she has much to learn, and it is to be hoped that we shall both enjoy the process.'

As the Condesa slowly relaxed against her mound of silk pillows and smiled a little to herself, Lise wasn't sure whether she was taken in by Leandro, or amused by the idea of a girl standing up to him. 'All the same it is only correct that a ring be given from her hand into yours, Leandro. I have a ring of your grandfather's which would be most suitable and if you will open the small safe behind El Conquistadore and bring to me the gold box which I keep inside, then we will ensure that the exchange of rings takes place as it should. It is not only an attractive custom, but it will convince me, Leandro, that you are sincere at last in your desire to take a wife and start a family. I shall very soon be eighty, and I wish to hold your son in my arms before I pass on to the beloved arms of your grandfather. Now go to my safe and bring the box, Leandro.'

'At your wish, Madrecita.' He spoke a trifle sardonically, and as he withdrew his arm from around Lise he seemed to let his fingers trail deliberately across her back. She almost jumped, for strangely alarming were the sensations he evoked, as if her skin would have liked him to go on touching her even as her mind rejected him. Her mind knew that he was playing a game, but her unawakened body knew only its own primitive reactions to a practised male touch.

He would have to stop touching her, she thought wildly. She had never met anyone like him before, and if she hoped to leave the *castillo* as puritan as she had entered it, then she must put a stop to physical contact with Leandro de Marcos Reyes. There was a sensual magnetism about the man that was as highly dangerous as going too close to a live wire, and though it was true that Lise had been devotedly guarded by a responsible brother, she was not so unworldly that she didn't know there was a hunger in everyone for the sublimation of body and spirit in the arms of another person.

She knew that it was called total surrender, and she felt herself go weak as water at the thought of such surrender in the strong, dark arms of this Spaniard who was using her to take his grandmother's attention off the woman he really wanted.

'Are you very much in love with him?' The question came suddenly, and Lise flinched as if from the flick of a whip-lash. She had been glad that Leandro had left the bedroom for a few minutes, but now she wanted him to return so that he could stand between her and such searching questions from the Condesa. She cast a quick glance at the door and prayed that he would appear before she had to answer his grandmother's inevitable question.

'Ah, I see that you are.' Her glance had been taken to mean that she couldn't wait for him to hurry back to her side, and when Lise dared to look at the Condesa she saw

85

that she was smiling to herself. 'How could it be otherwise when he has such a vital personality, and you are very obviously a girl who has not had a lot to do with men. I am pleased – very pleased indeed.'

And the Condesa was looking pleased when her grandson came back into the room carrying in his hands the gold box she had asked for. He placed it on the bed, and Lise felt the flickering look which he cast at her face, as if wondering what had been said to her during his short absence. She felt the turbulence of her own emotions, the pull against him, and the pull towards him, and it was infuriating, as if she were no longer in control of her own destiny while she remained within the radius of this man's personality. She was caught, held, twirled like a pin on a magnet, and because she felt a prisoner of his steel and velvet she cast him a resentful look, steeling her grey eyes to look cool and hostile.

He met her look and his brows joined in a black straight line, giving him a look of threat. Defiance thrilled through Lise and she stormily told herself that she would not be treated as if she were really bound to this – this imperious devil who didn't care if she got hurt so long as the Condesa and his darling Franquista emerged unscathed from his reckless game of chance.

'Here, child, take this ring and place it on the hand of Leandro!'

It was a most definite order, and short of an outright refusal, which would seem very odd, Lise could do nothing else but take the carved gold ring and avoid a direct meeting with Leandro's eyes as held out his hand so that she might slip the ring on the fourth finger. It glinted against his dark skin, and was set at its centre with a gleaming ruby.

'Now you will give your two hands to me.' The Condesa spoke with a very satisfied note in her voice. 'I wish to give my blessing to this engagement, for which an old woman

86

like me should not have had to wait so long. Your hand, Leandro! And now yours, my child!'

With a fuming reluctance Lise extended her left hand, adorned by the sapphire that was meant for someone who knew herself passionately loved, and she gave an uncontrollable shiver as the Condesa took her hand and placed it in that of her grandson. His lean, strong fingers closed about hers, holding them like a manacle, while his grandmother murmured some words in Spanish, and then crossed herself. Lise could feel her legs shaking, and her heart pounding. She almost felt that she would faint unless she escaped from this room, from these two people who were really strangers to her, and yet who seemed to be taking control of her life.

She had to be dreaming ... but the fingers holding hers were too real and warm to be part of a dream

'Go now, the two of you,' said the Condesa, and suddenly her face had a look of weariness, so that the paint on her cheeks seemed to take on the look of shrivelled petals. 'I have had much excitement this morning and must now take a little rest. Send Manuela to me so she can tidy up my bed, and put my jewel box back in the safe, Leandro. *Es bueno, mi novillo*, that you do this thing to please me.'

'What, put away your jewel box?' he said dryly.

At once the Condesa looked at him with a pair of flashing eyes. 'You know well enough what I mean. Now take the box and the girl, and leave me in peace.'

'*Lo que tu quieras, madrecita mia.*' He bent his tall head and kissed the temple of his grandmother. 'I am honoured to wear the ring of the man you greatly loved.'

'The ring is yours, *mio*. I meant always to give it to you.' She smiled tiredly. 'Today you have made me happy. I hope it is a gift I may hope to keep.'

And so saying she closed her eyes, and Lise escaped from the room ahead of Leandro, but with long strides he soon caught up with her on the bend of the stairs. She hastened, and panic was so blind in her at that moment that she didn't watch her step on the twisting stairs and she felt herself falling even as the man at her heels caught at her and swung her back into his arms to safety.

Safety? Could such a word be applied to finding herself, shaken and shocked in the arms of Leandro de Marcos Reyes, held close to the hard frame of him and almost on the verge of tears. 'Let me go!' she said, raggedly.

'So that you might stumble again and next time break your neck.' His arm was locked about her like a thing of steel, and with his left hand he pushed the fair hair back off her brow and held her so that she was forced to look at him. The tears of shock and silent fury were plain in her grey eyes, making them shimmer, making the lashes cling darkly about their wide, furious pleading.

'How could you let a lie go so far?' she demanded. 'It's devilish of you . . . allowing that exchange of rings, and then that bedside blessing I – I never agreed to anything like that. I just thought I'd have to meet the Condesa, and never dreamed of it becoming so – so serious. You will have to tell her the truth. You can't allow her to go on thinking that you – you and I are actually engaged. She knows already that you are intimate with Franquista—'

'Intimate?' He spoke the word so close to Lise's face that his breath was warm against her skin, imparting to the word a far more deeper meaning than she had meant to imply. 'What do you mean, my innocent young *inglesa*? Are you suggesting that I would dishonour a woman I happen to love? Or that I would bother to marry a woman I could dishonour? You have a lot to learn about me, haven't you?'

'A lot?' she gasped, straining away from him, and yet finding him illimitably stronger than she and able to gather

her back to him as if she were no more than a few yards of fine silk. It was an experience she had never had before, the discovery that a determined man was so very much stronger than a woman. She wanted to struggle and claw and escape at any cost, but he controlled her as effortlessly as a doll with sawdust limbs.

'You will only wear yourself out if you go on expending all this emotion and energy,' he drawled. 'You could at any time have blurted out to Madrecita that we were *both* frauds, but you let happen what did happen. You placed the ring on my finger, and you stood dumb as she gave us her blessing. If you hated it all so much, then why didn't you make your protest to her face? It would all be over now. You would be getting ready to leave th e castle and—'

'Oh, do stop it!' Lise broke in angrily. 'I could see what you can see each time you visit your grandmother. She puts on a good show of being the woman she probably was a few years ago, but we both felt the tremor to her hands, and saw the look of exhaustion under the rouge. She is still magnificent, but she is old and tired, and though I can't forgive you personally for the way you have involved me in your secret schemes, I can understand what drove you to the deception. If I had a grandmother like her, I might be tempted to do hateful things in order to spare her feelings. But it is a dangerous game! And I'm afraid of where it could lead!'

'Along the path to the altar?' He gave his deep, mocking laugh and buried his fingers deep under her hair. 'Would you find marriage with me so very hateful, little one? Think of living in a castle, and having a husband who could satisfy your every whim. You would be a *condesa* yourself, and no longer a girl who sews fine materials for the figures of other women. You would wear those fine fabrics yourself and emerge quite a stunning little butterfly from your chrysalis of the duty bound.'

'Stop it!' She twisted her head aside in an attempt to avoid his mocking eyes, and at once his fingers painfully gripped the nape of her neck and forced her into submission to his gaze. It travelled all over her face, taking in the young, pure line of her jaw and throat, made taut by the way he held her so that her skin showed its flawless texture. His gaze travelled to her ears, and to her eyes, both with a faun-slant to them, then drifted down again to her lips, the upper lip more finely drawn than the fuller lower lip.

Abruptly he bent his head and with a kind of indolent carelessness he brushed her lips with his. She hadn't dreamed that he would go this far and the shock of the action mingled with the sensation of feeling his warm lips blending with hers.

Young men had kissed her before, grabbing hold of her at staff parties and planting their ungainly kisses on her mouth ... but never had she known this type of expertise, this running of flame over the contours of her mouth ... this closeness of animal grace and dark, honeyed skin over the slope of Latin cheekbones. To try and blot out what was happening she closed her eyes, and as if he took this for a sign of surrender he placed his lips against her eyelids, and when she stirred wildly he took his lips to her left earlobe, and again those shock waves ran through her as she felt the bared edge of his teeth.

'Don't!' She cried out the word, and this time he allowed her to tear herself out of his arms and he stood there, showing the glinting edge of his teeth in a smile of pure devilment, while above his eyes a strand of black hair daggered his brow.

'Don't?' he mocked. 'But it is done, *pequeña*. You have been kissed by me, and even if you scrub your lips and face with antiseptic, you can't wipe away so easily the memory of the hateful contact. Hateful, of course, from your angle. Rather enticing from mine.'

'You're despicable!' she flung at him. 'You deceive your own grandmother and play about with other girls behind the back of the person you're supposed to be so in love with. I had been warned that Latin men were wolves, but I never dreamed that any one of them could be as bad as you.' She flung the hair back from her face, blending defiance with demand. 'I want to leave, *señor*. You can tell the Condesa we had a sudden row and I returned your ring.' So saying she wrenched at the sapphire, but to her consternation it wouldn't move beyond her knuckle. The golden band clung, and the sapphire burned, and she fought to remove the ring as Leandro leaned against the wall of the stairs and watched her, his eyelids half-lowered so that his regard took on a certain look of menace.

'I was forgetful of how small was my mother's hand,' he said. 'I shouldn't do that if I were you, Lise. You are going to make the knuckle swell and then nothing short of a jeweller's knife will remove the ring.'

'Soap will do it,' she rejoined. 'I shall go to my room and remove it there, and then if you will arrange to have my car fixed up, I shall be on my way.'

'I think not,' he said deliberately. 'You are committed to me for as long as I wish you to remain here, and if you jeopardise my grandmother's peace of mind and body in any way, then I promise that you will really learn what a Latin wolf can do to a small white lamb who has been foolhardy enough to stray from her shepherd. As for your car, it has been removed to a garage and I am informed by telephone that the spare part needed to put it back on the road will have to be sent from Madrid. It is an English make of car, remember, and isolated garages in the *sierras* do not stock many spare parts for the vehicles of foreign tourists. I do realize that European women consider the world their playground, and fancy it is stocked with only things and people to make life easier for them. But the truth is, *señorita*, this is Spain and a particularly out-of-the-way part of Iberia. And here *I* am in authority and I can make life pleasant or unpleasant for you, according to your choice.'

He paused and stared at her with those menacingly narrowed eyes. 'Well, Miss Harding, what is your choice? That of my pampered *novia*, or that of a young woman who broke a promise? You did promise to do this thing for me, and I am holding you to that promise.'

'You are pretty ruthless, Conde de Marcos Reyes,' she said gravely.

'Yes, ruthless, but not exactly pretty,' he mocked. 'Now leave that ring alone—'

'I wish you'd leave me alone,' she broke in, 'if only for a few hours. For heaven's sake allow me to adjust to this – this madhouse in the *sierras*.' A ragged little laugh escaped her. 'My sister-in-law warned me I couldn't come alone to Spain and hope to avoid trouble. I had to give Audrey and my brother the slip in order to—' Lise bit her lip. 'For now you seem to have the upper hand, *señor*, and I admit that I'm half to blame for the predicament in which I find myself. If I co-operate, will you do the same?'

'And what exactly does my co-operation entail?' he queried.

'No more kissing,' she blurted. 'It isn't part of the bargain, least of all without an audience to impress. It isn't fair—'

'It isn't meant to be fair,' he drawled. 'It is meant to be rather exciting. You are an oddly puritanical young person, aren't you? One hears so much about the liberated English Miss, with her forthright views on life and love, but the moment she is thrown into contact with a man she develops all the symptoms of cold feet and palpitations. Well, for my part I am not displeased. I should not want – even deceptively – an English fiancée who was as liberated as some of them appear to be on the beaches of Spain.'

He took a step towards her and when she backed away, dangerously close to the stairs down which she had almost tripped a while ago, he quickly gripped her wrist and she gave a little cry at the ungentle pressure of his fingers.

'Your neck is too pretty to be broken by a flight of stairs. Come, I will see you to your suite, where you can take a rest from all this turmoil of the emotions.'

His hand slid warm to her elbow, and once again Lise had to give in to his command. He seemed thoroughly gifted for getting his own way, and any show of opposition only left Lise feeling as physically and emotionally bruised as a bird which kept battering its wings against the bars of its cage.

No kisses, she had pleaded, but he had made no promise to abide by her plea, and she just couldn't bring herself to touch on the subject again. He made her feel too humiliatingly callow . . . as if she believed that a kiss was meant to indicate affection. On his part it had meant no more than a subtle torment, an inquisitive wish to explore her lack of experience. She told herself she hated him for that . . . alone in her room she insisted to herself that he was hateful.

She walked out to the veranda and the sun played in the heart of the sapphire as she clenched her hands over the iron-laced parapet. Had his mother's reaction been similar to hers when that other *conde* had placed the ring on her hand? Lise gnawed her lip and gazed at the blue blaze of the gem. If she could have wrenched off the ring she would in her temper have thrown it at Leandro's face. He had no right . . . no right at all to kiss her.

Her heart pounded as she stood there, and again that curious weakness swept over her as she recalled the electrical contact with his lips. She didn't dare to think beyond a kiss, and she forced herself to study her surroundings, letting her gaze rise to the heights of the *sierras*, with their mantling of snow merging with the sky.

Up there the crags of rock were barren of foliage, but lower down there were dense masses of silvery-green vegetation and Lise guessed that it was a plantation of olive trees ... and then as she gazed at the slopes there came to her the sound of bells pealing in a belfry, clear and strangely sweet, and carried she supposed on the wind that would always blow around those peaks, so that the olive trees dwelt under the protection of the tall eucalyptus trees.

Suddenly a bird flew close to Lise's veranda and settled with a cooing sound on the iron parapet. It strutted there as if well aware that it had nothing to fear, and it was beautiful, a dove plumaged with turquoise-blue feathers.

Lise now realized why this apartment had been occupied by the Conde's mother. From here could be heard the bells of possibly a mountain chapel, and doves came unafraid to the veranda. But they were free to fly if something should alarm them ... it was Lise who was the caged dove in the castle of the hawk.

CHAPTER FIVE

PERHAPS it was the doves and the bells which helped to win Lise over to the undeniable attraction of El Serafin, and in the next few days the Conde did nothing too drastic to ruffle her feathers. She grew almost accustomed to having breakfast served on a sunlit patio surrounded by scented plants to the music of a graceful stone fountain fed from a spring that piped snow-water all the way down from the mountains. That combination of cool water and hot sunshine splashing through the ferny palms was entrancing.

The patio was entered through a *puerta de la luna,* a moon door, and each morning Lise had a sense of stepping into a picture, with coloured tiles underfoot leading to the plaited-cane table set beneath the magenta blaze of a bougainvillea.

And there she was served breakfast, for the most part alone, for Ana went off early to chapel, and to visit in the village, while the Conde had various tasks to attend to about the *castillo.* Being a very old place, carefully preserved, it had to be checked on to make sure the floors and beams were not being invaded by parasites. That the stonework was not giving away anywhere, and there was no sign of dampness in the cellars. It seemed that over the years Leandro had become an expert on the preservation of his inheritance, and Ana said that he was determined not to let such a fine old castle fall into ruin as so many other Spanish castles had fallen. It took a lot of money, of course, to keep it in order, and to maintain a staff at good salaries, but the family business in Madrid, with factories in other parts of Spain, was a flourishing one, and to date there seemed no reason why the *castillo* should not be preserved as the family residence. Leandro had a fine apartment in Madrid, but that was not the same as being able to come to the country to ride his horses and enjoy his olive plantation. And it would surely break the Condesa's heart if she ever had to leave El Serafin.

'The Condesa and the *castillo* mean a lot to Leandro,' Ana one day confided. 'As a boy he was aware that his parents were not happy together, and it was an open secret that the Conde his father had a mistress at Granada. She was a dancer of *flamenco*, and so she had gipsy blood in her veins. Leandro adored his mother, so it was not a good thing for him to learn, that when his father was absent from home he was at Granada with this other woman. He was not a man for business and in those days a general manager was in charge.' Ana had flushed slightly. 'He was the father of Chano Velarde, as it happens, and that is how it is that Chano is such a close associate of the present *conde*. They were always much together as boys and young men, and were only separated when Leandro went to England to complete his education. I believe the Condesa feared for him to have the *flamenco* contacts which his father had at the University of Granada. Later on that dancer was the cause of his father's death, for she was driving his car very fast when it crashed and they were both killed. She, they say, not outright. It was very terrible. She was found in the wreckage, still conscious then, and sightless, her lovely dark face in ruins, holding in her lap the dead body of the Conde. Madrina has always feared that the tragedy would repeat itself, but now—'

Ana had smiled with such trust at Lise. 'Now we are happy that he, the grandson who is her very life, has an English girl like you for his *novia*. Madrina's mind is set at rest, praise be.'

Lise tried, after this conversation, not to think of the future. She set herself to enjoy each hour, each day as it came, and no day could start more colourfully than hers did at El Serafin. She had quickly established the fact that she didn't wish to have breakfast in bed, and when she discovered the little patio beyond the moon door she asked at once if it would be all right for her to have breakfast there.

The *alma de llaves*, who was in charge of the household, was quite taken aback that Lise should actually ask if it was all right. 'It is for the *señorita* to give her orders and for us to carry them out,' was the reply. 'The *señorita* is to be wife of the Conde and he would be annoyed if we did not make you as happy as it is within our power to do so. The *señorita* will, of course, wish for an English breakfast, and Florentina will be most happy to oblige.'

And so it was that Lise enjoyed her own pot of tea each morning, served with scrambled or boiled eggs, thick slices of mountain cured ham, crisp rolls, gorgeous thick marmalade made from local oranges, and always a different sort of fruit. Lise felt as if she were being treated like a princess, and she would have been a most unnatural girl if she had not enjoyed the spoiling. For years as a working girl she had rushed through breakfast in order to catch the bus, and then the underground train to Kensington, and it was delightful to eat perfect food in a Spanish garden, and to have the leisure to enjoy the sun and the sound of the birds.

El Serafin was rather heavenly . . . if only she had been a guest here instead of the Conde's fake fiancée. She would have loved all this, instead of feeling in a false position all the time.

At first she felt reluctant to explore the castle, but curiosity took her in its grip and she found herself seeking out the various rooms, the galleries and small chambers tucked away in odd corners. She discovered paintings and tapestries that gave her a picture of what Spanish life must have been like in days gone by. She entered a scarlet-carpeted *sala* and gazed in wonder at the high coffered ceiling painted in the Moorish style and hung with immense lamps of oriental design. Here there was a dark, passionate whisper of the Moorish past, with divans overlaid with rich silks, and carpets of woven silk hanging upon the smooth white walls. There were cabinets of richly carved wood in which were displayed the barbaric ornaments and daggers from the days when this Iberian family had mingled its history with that of a hawkish Saracen.

Lise was no longer in any doubt about the strain of ruthlessness in Leandro de Marcos Reyes. She wandered about the wonderful old *sala* and she came to understand why he and his father had been drawn to darkly passionate women. The old, old desires lingered in their blood and the Condesa knew of this, and she had tried to eradicate it, first with a dove-like bride from a convent, and then by her adoption of Ana, who she had hoped would please Leandro.

Lise paused in front of a cabinet on whose velvet-lined shelves lay the jewellery which must long ago have adorned a woman of greed and beauty. The gems in the bracelets were huge and must have weighed down the arms of the wearer, and there were yard-long necklaces that must have reached to the girl's ankles, where once again she would have been chained by bands of gold ornamented with jewels. Her ankles, earlobes and breast would have sparkled and jingled as she walked. The odalisque of the oriental dream . . . haunting, thought Lise, the imagination of the man who had asked *her* of all people to pose as the future provider of his earthly paradise.

She was standing thus in the colourful *sala*, laughing softly and incredulously to herself, when a voice spoke at her elbow and she almost jumped out of her skin – lightly covered in one of the silk shifts she had made for herself out of the wonderful range of fabrics which Leandro had presented to her.

'*Buenas tardes, señorita,* do I have the pleasure of speaking to the fiancée of my friend the Conde?'

She swung round to face the speaker, and found him to be lean, dark, and extremely good-looking. The perfect Latin, with well-made features and clad in a dark suit of impeccable cut, with a tiny red flower in the lapel of his jacket. His eyes looking into hers were grave for a moment, and then he slowly smiled, and Lise liked him immediately, without a shadow of reservation. There was in his smile the kindness of a good heart, and she suspected who he was before he inclined his dark head and lightly clicked his heels.

'I am Chano Velarde, at your service, *señorita.* I have just come from Madrid, and you have, perhaps, been told of me.'

'I have, indeed, Señor Velarde.' Lise broke into a smile herself and held out a hand to him. 'I am pleased to meet you, *señor.* I feel I know you already – from Ana.'

He took her hand and his fingers were strong and yet so much gentler than Leandro's. 'I am delighted to meet you, *señorita.*' His eyes held a gleam of laughter looking into hers. 'I had heard you spoken of once or twice, but I really began to believe that you must be a figment of Leandro's imagination; someone he invented in order to keep the Condesa at bay in her attempts to change him from a bachelor to a married man. But now I see that you are very real, and even prettier than the Conde led us all to believe. He would never tell me the exact colour of his *novia*'s eyes, and I used to tease him by saying that the man who cannot recall the colour of his *amiga*'s eyes is a man not truly in love. Now I see why he kept so many details to himself. He comes of a line who many years ago kept their women from the eyes of other men. They were the *hidalgos* who believed in the *mirador*, the enclosed balcony behind which only the veiled and mysterious shape of the lady could be glimpsed.'

Lise gave a little laugh and gestured around the *sala*. 'I have just discovered the dash of the Moor in my – in Leandro. Isn't this a fascinating room? Rather like a museum to which each generation of the family has added its bit of history. Look at this lovely lacework, and these gorgeous fans and combs. And these miniatures and tiny boxes of jade and silver must be priceless. They take my breath away.'

'What of the jewellery?' he asked. 'Don't you fancy wearing any of that?'

'One would have to be statuesque, or weighed to the ground by its sheer luxuriance. Was that the idea, I wonder? To have the woman at the feet of her master?'

'I should imagine that was very much the idea – in days gone by.' Chano spoke dryly, and yet with a note of meaning in his voice. 'I think it might put your mind at rest if I say that I believe Leandro to be a trifle more emancipated in his views. The very fact that he has become engaged to a British girl would verify my belief. After all, the British do not go along with the idea of the enslaved woman, do they? Some of our business associates come from England and their wives seem free to do whatever pleases them.'

'I don't think you are quite in accord with that idea.' Lise had noticed the slight hardening of his mouth, and the puckering of his dark brows, as if as a Latin he could never allow his own wife the freedom to flirt with other men. She knew instinctively that it was that aspect of the marital relationship to which he referred, and being English herself she well knew that it was no longer considered not quite the thing for married couples to stray outside the bonds of their wedlock. If a girl went to a party in England she was more likely to be propositioned by a married man than a single one. Chano would know of this, as he had visited England. And so would Leandro. It must therefore strike Chano and other people he knew as strange that he should introduce an English girl as his wife to be.

She studied Chano and wondered if he knew about Franquista. Somehow she had the feeling that he didn't quite believe in Leandro's engagement to herself. But she also knew that he was loyal to the family and he would play the game, if Leandro wanted it that way. It might also suit him to do so ... if he were attracted to Ana and had hopes of winning her for himself

'Will you be staying at the castle, *señor*?' she asked, and interest in him and Ana brightened her eyes and brought a warm lilt to her voice. Suddenly it seemed important that at least one girl at the castle should find romance and happiness with a rather dashing man.

'Yes, I am here for a few days to have some private talks to Leandro about the new factory we are thinking of opening just outside Malaga, where the chance of employment slackens off when the wine-making season is over. Now that so much machinery is used in the production of the wine, less and less people are required to do the manual labour, so Leandro thought it might be a good idea to start a factory there – but you don't wish to hear all this dry business talk!'

'On the contrary, *señor*, I am most interested,' Lise assured him. 'It's nice to hear that the Conde is concerned for the welfare of poor people.'

'He is not a selfish man, for all that he has grown up with privilege,' Chano said warmly. 'But all the same I should not really talk of this matter until it is settled. The Latin, *señorita*, is a little secretive because he is rather superstitious, and we believe that the Devil listens in to our schemes and our dreams, and so we throw him off the scent by talking of other things. Tell me, what do you think of the *castillo*?'

'It is like something out of a fable,' she smiled. 'I never believed that such a place could exist in this day and age.'

'Did not Leandro tell you about it, when you met in England?' There was again that slightly droll note in Chano's voice. 'But perhaps you imagined it as run-down and going to ruin, as so many Spanish castles, alas, are going through dwindling funds and high taxation.'

'It would be a great pity if such a fabulous place was neglected, and then again the Condesa is so fond of it.' Lise spoke in a matter-of-fact voice, as if unaware that this close associate and friend of the Conde suspected a conspiracy aimed at keeping the Condesa from her matchmaking.

'And what do you make of the matriarch?' he asked. 'She has a reputation for greatly alarming the timid, but I don't think you are a timid girl, eh?'

'I hope not! I have now met the Condesa a couple of times and we have managed to get along quite well. She is still very fascinating, and she likes to talk about her youthful conquests and I like to listen. It must have been enormously romantic to be courted below a balcony, to the music of a guitar. She told me that one evening alone she collected seven different flowers from seven different men. Romance seems to have died out in my country, but here in Spain one seems to hear an echo of it, and to glimpse it in the flash of a girl's eyes over a fan.'

'So you like Spain, *señorita*?'

'Yes – very much.' For the first time Lise realized the total truth of those words. A love of this country had come alive in her heart, and though it would no longer be possible for her to work for Franquista when she left the castle and was free to continue with her normal life, there were other cities in Spain to which she could go in search of her own sort of work. Leandro had offered her money and she might accept it and open a small shop of her own. The prospect was quite exciting, and if the shop proved a success she would be able to pay back the money and be entirely independent.

'I understand that Ana is on one of her errands of mercy down in the village,' said Chano. 'I have my car and I wonder if you would care for a drive? We can pick up Ana and bring her back with us.'

'I'd enjoy that very much, *señor*. I'll just go and powder my nose and meet you down in the forecourt.'

'Don't forget *un sombrero*. My car is an open one, the sun is hot, and you are fair-skinned. I should not wish to give sunstroke to Leandro's girl.'

'I'll be sure to fetch a hat.' Lise left him quickly, turning away before he saw the colour rise vividly to her cheekbones. In her room she changed into pale-coloured slacks and a pale-green shirt, and after powdering over the flush that lingered high on her cheeks, she snatched up the wide-brimmed straw hat, given to her the other day by Ana, and made her way downstairs. By the time she reached the car she looked cool and ready for a drive, and was rather taken with the shining petrol-blue colour of the smart little roadster.

As if by mutual, unspoken consent neither of them mentioned the Conde again, and as the car made its smooth way down the winding cliff road, Lise caught a dazzling glimpse of the sea and said at once that she had been looking forward to a swim and perhaps Chano would persuade Ana to take time off from her self-imposed welfare work so that the three of them could enjoy, perhaps, a picnic on the beach.

'Ana is a little earnest for a young girl,' he laughed softly. 'I have never interfered because there was always the chance that – to put it frankly – she might be the next young *condesa*. But now I shall persuade her to relax while I am here. She must realize that I find her pretty, and there is time enough for a pretty girl to become a woman of cares and duties. I notice, *señorita*, that you have not yet taken up the basket and the bandage.'

'Do call me Lise.' She laughed a little, and breathed the pure mountain air. 'I am on holiday, *señor*, and do my share of work when the holidays are at an end. I have an idea Ana gets rather bored. She is a much more maternal person than I am, and I am sure she thoroughly enjoys looking after some of those lovely Latin babies down in the village. There is a madonna quality about Ana. She will make some man a lovely wife.'

And as if her words made a deep impression on Chano, he drove for some time in silence, and when they reached the stretch of road at the base of the mountains, Lise settled back to enjoy the countryside through which they sped. Here and there the sienna-coloured land was shaded by a great fig tree, a filigree of branches against a hot sky, where now and then a hawk circled with wide-spread wings, again a wild and lovely shape etched by sun and space. Now and again they passed a rambling *cortijo*, with high hedges of prickly pear to keep marauding wild game from the fruit orchards and the olive yards. The white walls of these farmhouses could be glimpsed beyond the hedges, and sometimes a shady old courtyard aflame with the dark blaze of geraniums.

In sunlight these lonely farms were picturesque, but Lise wondered what it was like to be an occupant when a storm came down from the high *sierras* and the violet lightning flashed across the land. One could never forget that the mountains were there, powerful and brooding, like great monarchs of stone that watched the world below, and made the village seem toylike, cradled there in a swooping arc of rock.

This was the first time Lise had been to the village, and so clear and golden was the light of the day that each small house seemed like a painting against the towering, multi-green frame of the mountains.

Some walls were the colour of pomegranates, while others were crusted in leaf and undulant flowering vines, rising to red tiles laid in neat rows on the sloping roof. There was a Moorish sculpturing to doorways, in contrast to the carved golden cross above the white narrow steeple of the convent hospital, where Ana came to assist with the new babies, and the small children confined to the long white ward for a while.

The most impressive part of the village was the miniature plaza, as gorgeously tiled as if in Madrid itself, set round with trees, and with a fine old fountain at its centre. The tang of rosemary hung on the air, and Lise was told by Chano that the local bakers used it in their ovens for fuel, for it grew so abundantly on the mountain slopes that great bundles of it were collected and brought in on the backs of donkeys.

That heavy, tangy perfume hung on the afternoon air as Chano drove right through the village so he could park his car in the shade of an old Arab tower that lingered here from the days of Moorish occupation. The tower was of dark ruby stone, probably hacked out of the mountains and designed to linger, as the dark, oriental gleam lingered in the eyes of the people of El Serafin.

When they left the car the two of them stood a moment, absorbing the lost-in-time beauty of the place. 'Yes,' murmured Chano, as if sensing her thoughts. 'Stone and granite was hauled up the cliffside for the building of the castle, and probably many of the ancestors of these villagers did the work. Nothing of beauty comes without the toil of men, and the imagination of women.'

' "*The splendour falls on castle walls, And snowy summits old in story,*" ' quoted Lise. 'This place, and one's awareness of the *castillo* up there in the mountains, makes Tennyson come alive. I often felt that he couldn't have been thinking of an English castle when he wrote that poem.'

'I think,' said Chano, as they began to stroll towards the plaza, 'that certain of the English are very sensitive to our landscape, and even to our history. I think already that you feel drawn to El Serafin and its people. In many ways they live an old-fashioned life, and are content with it, and that is why Leandro, who is veritable liege lord of the place, refuses to allow a hotel to be built here. Tourists would expect gift shops, swimming pools, probably a funicular into the mountains, and in no time at all the people of El Serafin would be thinking only of the money to be made out of the visitors, and they would absorb some of the bored restlessness of these tourists and become discontented themselves. It is Leandro's business to consider the well-being of his people, and think how changed this delightful place would become if it were discovered by the holidaymakers.'

The idea made Lise wince, for there was such grace to the old stone houses about the *plaza*, shaded by rose-flowered oleanders, and spike-shadowed palms. Morning glory trailed over the cloisters of the convent hospital, and when they entered under the archway, Lise caught her breath at the ripening apricot and plum trees, and the almost golden lustre of the tiles that inlaid the interior of the courtyard. A Judas tree had laced itself to another with velvety purple leaves, and there were tile-covered benches set beneath these trees which must have been as old as the convent itself.

The white walls were sun-patched, and small square windows had green shutters to shade them, and rising above the building was the bell-tower itself, a lovely, graceful thing of open-sided arcades that would carry the sound of the bells all over the village and up the slopes of the cliffs.

'This is the Convento de Vista del Sol,' said Chano. 'The exterior has been kept as it always was, but Leandro has ensured that everything inside is up-to-date for the very best benefit of the patients. The good Sisters learn their nursing at one of the best hospitals in Madrid, and their chief surgeon is fortunately a man who cares more about country people than making a fortune among the rich, whose main ailment is very often over-indulgence. A man such as Leandro is saved from such a life by his many responsibilities, but his father before him was not quite so dutiful.'

Chano shrugged and reached a hand to a cloak of tiny waxen white flowers that gave off a scent like honeysuckle. 'It may have been because he married the wrong woman. There is no doubt that the right person in one's life can make all the difference. Bodies can be attracted, but it is also essential that two souls are in accord. Do you not agree, *señorita*?'

'It's a very profound question, *señor*. And a very demanding sort of love. I – I haven't really thought in those depths just yet.' Then she bit her lip, realizing how she gave herself away. 'Shall we go and look for Ana? Are we allowed into the hospital?'

'Yes.' The look he gave her was rather grave, as if the atmosphere of the convent made it seem very wrong that she and Leandro might not be genuinely in love with each other.

'Do we go this way?' She hastened towards one of the arched entrances and was acutely relieved when she saw Ana coming out into the sunshine.

'I saw you both from a window!' Ana's eyes were shining, and for once her dark hair was loose about her face, as if she had been romping with some of the young patients. Lise had not yet seen her looking so young and happy. 'Chano! How good to see you!'

'How very good to see you, *pequeña*!' He caught at Ana's hands and carried them to his lips, and when the girl blushed like a rose, Lise knew for certain that she cared for Chano . . . had probably cared for him a long time, but had felt duty bound to have her life arranged by the Condesa.

Lise smiled to herself, and forgot for a moment that wild, restless feeling of guilt which had swept over her. Well, if her presence at El Serafin achieved happiness for these two, then she need not feel too much of a fraud. Ana certainly looked as if the sun was shining from her eyes, and Chano was holding her hands as if he wished to carry her off there and then.

'If you are finished here for the day, then we will drive you back to the castle,' he said. 'Do you know, Ana, if it is possible you are even prettier than when last I saw you. And so grown up!'

'*Gracias*, Chano, for the compliment. But my hair feels terribly untidy—'

'It looks terribly nice like that,' Lise broke in. 'Young and carefree, and you must keep it that way instead of pulling it back in a severe knot. Don't you agree, Chano?'

'I most certainly do agree. Now before driving back, as it is about four o'clock and the café on the plaza will be opening, shall we have some refreshments? And perhaps some of those delicious *churros* which are never so good in the city, being half burnt most of the time. *Dios*, city life is so fast and furious these days, and it really is good to get to the country where the air is fresh and alive, and the girls look as sweet as the fruit on the trees. Come! Let us go and feed our faces.'

With eager steps they made their way to the *plaza*, where

the café tables were shaded by parasols, and where the oleanders and palms threw their shadows on the polished tiles of the pavement. Other people were drifting in the same direction, and a tang of coffee stole from the open doorway of the café, as if beckoning to the passer-by.

They sat down at a table for three, and at once the waiter came to take their order – iced tangerine cordial, and a plate of *churros*, golden and sugared and crunchy.

Chano then leaned back in his cane chair and studied his two companions, so much a contrast to each other. Ana so raven-haired and clad in a garnet-red slipover, with a bishop-sleeved blouse underneath. And Lise bare-armed in a pale-green shirt, her slacks tapered to her long legs, her earlobes nude of tiny golden rings under her sunlit hair. Most Latin girls had these gold rings pierced into their earlobes at a very young age, and over the years it was possible for them to be interchanged with all kinds of hoops and drops, and buttons of pearl and turquoise and other jewels that looked stunning against the rich dark Latin hair.

Lise saw Chano's eyes upon the tiny gold rings in the earlobes of Ana, and she knew exactly what he was thinking ... that he would love to put sparkling gems in their place.

Instinctively Lise withdrew her left hand to her lap, dominated as it was by that sapphire which meant exactly nothing in terms of love and desire, and was being used by Leandro to convince his grandmother of a lie.

'Tomorrow I am coming with you to the hospital, Ana.' Lise spoke gaily, but anyone who knew her well would have noticed that her grey eyes were cloudy. 'I want to meet the children and be of some help myself.'

'Ah,' Chano held up his hand, 'but I am going to insist that Ana takes a holiday from the hospital while I am here at El Serafin. It will not be all business for me, and I shall need to be entertained. Well, Ana? What do you say? Are you going to turn me down?'

Ana looked at him in some confusion, then she appealed to Lise with a swift glance. 'Be a devil for once,' Lise laughed. 'All duty and no play makes a girl feel – uninteresting, as if she is taken for granted, like a piece of useful furniture which is there when needed, but unnoticed for a good deal of the time. Do you see?'

'Yes, I think I do see.' Ana ceased to tidy her hair with her hand and she stared at Chano Velarde as if suddenly aware that he was more than a charming business associate of the Conde's; he was a good-looking bachelor who was actually inviting her to use her charms on him, and she caught her breath at the thrill of the realization. 'Chano!' she gasped.

'Yes, that is my name,' he chuckled. 'Ah, and here comes our cool drinks and our crisp *churros*.'

A carefree hour followed, and when at last they made for the car, the sky was beginning to turn pink and purple above the peaks of the *sierras*. There were goats in the fields as they drove home to the castle, nibbling at the stalks of lavender and thyme. It was a magical and lovely scene, that would melt into the strange, almost melancholy beauty of the mountain night. *Noche triste*, and smoke rising from the logs that were lit in the great fireplace of the hall, the clumps of burning genista and twigs of rosemary giving out a scent that mingled with that of coffee and cognac. The tall figure of the Conde was reflected in the gold-rimmed mirrors, and the Condesa ate delicious convent-made sweets that were wrapped in silver paper. And then when the little silver clock chimed, Leandro would assist Madrecita from her velvet chair, and Lise would kiss her cheek, and the Condesa would go to her room, leaving in the air, with the scented smoke, those lovely Spanish words:

'With God, until tomorrow.'

The wind blew Lise's hair from her brow, for she held her straw hat on her lap, and she felt terribly glad that for the next few evenings Chano would be at the *castillo* to help relieve the tension of that after-dinner hour, when Lise was never certain what kind of question the Condesa would spring at her. And Lise was constantly aware of Leandro's own tension; his tiger-like readiness to intercept those sudden and unsettling questions, pouncing smoothly between the asking and the answering.

'You must decide on a date for the marriage,' the Condesa had said last night, 'I insist on that, Leandro. You must remember, *mio*, that I could go to my bed tonight and not awake tomorrow. I am an old woman and all my desires are gone – except the one, that I live to see you married in the cathedral at Jaen, where I was married to your grandfather. Is it so much to ask, that you name a day for wedding bells, before they toll the mourning bells?'

'You are eternally young,' he had retorted, 'but I promise you that soon I shall discuss the matter with the one I want for my wife.'

And last night he had lifted his *madrecita* into his arms and he had carried her off to her bed. And as the mountain winds blew against Lise's face, she recalled vividly the look there had been on his face, so that each feature had seemed sculptured in dark, rather tortured bronze. His eyes had swept Lise's face in passing, and their darkness had been impenetrable ... like a night without hope of stars.

The car of Chano Velarde reached the carved iron gates of the castle, not yet closed for the night, and as they sped along the tree-lined drive, Ana laughed softly at something Chano said to her, and a sudden bleak sense of loneliness swept over Lise. She, who was supposed to be the *novia* of Leandro de Marcos Reyes, was really the outsider ... the stranger burdened with a secret that was weighing on her heart as the great blue sapphire weighed on her hand.

The car came to a halt in the forecourt, below the ornamented stone corbels supporting the circular balconies of the twin towers. They stood below the steps leading to the boldly sculptured entrance, above which were carved some more of those seductive Spanish words, striking at the heart, and yet leaving the stranger to wonder if they were really meant to be taken seriously:

Mi casa es tu casa. My house is yours!

The lights were ablaze in the hall as they entered the castle. On a side table stood a cigar-box of embossed leather, and Chano paused to help himself to one of the thin, dark, strongly aromatic cigars. He crackled it in his fingers, then stabbed the end with the tiny silver instrument provided for this purpose, and applied the lighter-flame until the smoke streamed from his nostrils, and Lise had that choking, panicky sensation she had had last night . . . that feeling that she had to get away, if only to her room.

'I must dash and change for dinner.' She tried to control her voice, but it shook, strangely. 'Many thanks for a really enjoyable afternoon, *señor*. The village of El Serafin is an enchanting place, and I agree that it must never be spoiled.'

'It never will be while I am master here.' The words rang out crisply, and Lise had whirled about before she could stop herself. Leandro had just emerged from his leather-lined office, and his black hair was rumpled above his brow, as if while he did his accounts his hand had strayed in thought and reckoning through the thick, close waves. He wore a striped silk shirt open at the throat and dark corded trousers, held snug around his middle by a thin leather belt. There was a certain informality about his appearance that struck Lise as alarmingly attractive.

'I take it, Chano, that you have been showing Lise the *pueblo*? *La mar de gracias*, eh? And certainly not on the agenda for change.' The bite to his words made Lise look at his lips, and she saw their inflexibility, and their touch of arrogance, she knew that once he had set his mind on something, there would be no way to change his purpose ... short of killing him. As informally charming as he looked at the moment, she glimpsed the steel in him, and felt a cold shiver run all down her spine.

'It's a wonderful place, Leandro.' She spoke his name for the first time without hesitancy, despite that chilling little feeling that he could be savage if opposed over an issue which he took to heart. 'I have never in my life seen anything so – so perfect. I do agree that it must not be spoiled by tourist trespass.'

'No,' he agreed, and his eyes looked directly into hers, as if reminding her that when they had met she had been on her way there as a tourist. 'In a way we remain rather feudal at El Serafin. Those we do let in sometimes become so captivated that they want never to leave. There is a sense of *duende*, a mysterious charm that holds the heart a prisoner. Here we do not feel what is prevalent elsewhere, the longing for what is lost. *Anoranza. Muy interesante*, no?'

'Wonderfully interesting,' she agreed, and could feel her heart beating strangely fast as she turned with a gay smile at Ana. 'Shall we leave the men to smoke those fearfully strong cigars while we go and change for dinner?'

'We will see you both later,' smiled Chano, and with Latin courtesy he escorted them to the stairs, while Leandro lounged against the side table, lighting a cigar so the tiny flame leapt and reflected devilishly in his eyes. Lise could feel his eyes upon her as she started up the stairs, and she had the sure feeling that when he had talked about El

Serafin holding the heart a prisoner he had been referring to her heart.

When she parted from Ana and reached the seclusion of her own rooms that feeling felt intensified when she glanced around her bedroom and saw the circular shape of the walls.

She mustn't let her imagination play tricks with her . . . but all at once she felt as if she were a captive in a Spanish tower.

CHAPTER SIX

IN the quiet hour, before it was necessary to go downstairs, Lise finished sewing the hem of the dress she had made from a length of the deliciously soft rose-red silk which had come from the looms of the family factories. She studied each detail of the simple yet effective design, and then covered the small electric sewing-machine which Manuela had been kind enough to lend her.

The Condesa's companion had been curious, of course, as to why Lise should need to make frocks when everyone thought that she had come on an arranged visit to the castle. Lise had then found it necessary to resort to the excuse which Leandro had suggested; that her luggage had some-how got delayed in its arrival from Madrid.

'Why did you not bring it with you in the *señor's* car?' Manuela had asked.

Lise had been absolutely lost for an answer until she re-membered the golfing gear which had been stowed in the back of the Conde's car and the crate of champagne which had been unloaded from the boot in anticipation of the party in honour of his grandmother's birthday.

'You know what men are,' she had smiled, partly from the relief of having a good excuse to offer. 'They like to pretend that they can carry all they need in their pockets, but the truth of the matter was that Leandro was so loaded down with his own belongings that there just wasn't room for mine, except for a small case.'

Manuela had accepted this explanation, and had probably carried it to the Condesa. Anyway, nothing more had been remarked on the matter and the loan of the sewing-machine had been quickly forthcoming.

The rose-coloured dress was designed so that it left Lise's throat and arms bare, and was classically draped to her ankles, where the folds of the soft material tightened. Evening shoes would have proved a problem had it not occurred to Lise to cover a pair of canvas casuals with gold velvet. The result was highly attractive, and she discovered that walking in such shoes while wearing a long, close-fitting skirt gave her a lithe, catlike tread.

She had reached the foot of the stairs and was about to cross to the door of the *sala*, where they gathered for aperitifs before going into dinner, when she noticed that the door of the splendidly neglected castle ballroom was ajar, and in her present rather feline mood the enticement was too much for her and she had sped in the direction of the ballroom almost before she could stop herself and had slipped inside with the silence of a young cat. Beyond the uncurtained windows the moon was shining and the tide of its reflection was caught and held on the surfaces of the long mirrors lining the walls. The effect was one of dark silver and velvet, and feeling as buoyant and unknown as a shadow herself Lise sped to the centre of the vast room that was never used these days for the parties the Condesa would have loved when she was in the heyday of her beauty.

As if hearing the inviting music again, as if feeling the arms of an invisible partner, Lise danced the length of the ballroom, the silk of her dress whispering as she moved, the pale gleam of her hair caught and held by the gleam of the moon and the mirrors.

When the chandeliers sprang their shock of dazzling light, Lise was caught and held in her dancing attitude like a moth whirling into a flame.

'*Muy guapa*,' drawled a deep voice, and when Lise heard that voice she stood there burning, and wondered at her own idiocy in dancing by herself in the dark. Her mood that had been so strangely exalted was now at the mercy of Leandro's mockery, and she felt furious with him for coming upon her, and flicking on those great clusters of lights, and seeing her like a child caught play-acting.

She had felt so divinely young and free, whirling and twirling on this vast floor of polished tiles.

'It must be a certain whisper of the Moorish past that makes a girl so British a dancer for a long-dead lord of the harem.' Leandro came to the centre of the room, and Lise tensed as his footfalls rang on the glowing tiles. She could sense every muscle and bone of him, smoothly encased in his black tuxedo and trousers like a sword in its sheath. She could feel his dark eyes upon her body, sheathed in the rose-silk that had been his casual gift of the other day.

' *"Through what wild centuries roves back the rose."* ' As he spoke the words he reached the place where she stood, and the second stunning shock was the feel of his hands upon her waist, settling there, and then tightening, and twisting her to face him as effortlessly as if she had been made of petals and scent. 'I am thankful, *guapa*, that you have no actual thorns budding from this slender stem of yours. But the invisible thorns are bristling, are they not?'

She looked up at his face and saw the caressive cruelty of his mouth ... lips that demanded submission to strong kisses ... lips that could say words that stabbed and stroked.

'I – I know you think me an idiot,' she said stiffly, 'but these large rooms go a little to my head. They are so grand, and so lonely, somehow, as if begging someone to make a movement or a sound in them. I imagined there were grand parties when the Condesa was a younger woman. A woman as lovely and lively as she must have been would have enjoyed company.'

117

'She still enjoys company, but too much of it is not good for her these days.' He gazed down intently at Lise, and then he shifted his grip to her hands and holding them he drew away from her and studied her under the chandeliers. 'That is one of the dresses you have made and sewn yourself? You really are a clever child, and it seems a pity—'

'A pity, *señor*?' She could feel his fingers pressing against the fine bones of her wrists, holding her lightly but so surely, while his eyes travelled over. Under the fine silk she could feel how fast her heart was beating, and how strangely weak her legs felt when his gaze rested on the pale hollow of her throat.

'That such talent should be put to the service of another person,' he said. 'I must think about setting you up in a dress shop of your own – when the time comes. You would like that, Lise?'

'It would be too much to ask—'

'Nonsense.' He smiled, and this time without the slightest shading of mockery around his lips. 'I said at the start that you must have what is closest to your heart, did I not? Anyway, the time has not yet come for a discussion on that subject, and I have the feeling that Madrecita would expect me to add a little adornment to that white neck of yours. Come with me!'

'No!' Protest was so strong in Lise in that moment that she had to cry out against these attempts of his to smooth over the false situation by offering gifts. 'I won't!'

'But I can make you, my dear.' In an instant the mockery was back, twisting the edge of his mouth and glittering in his eyes. 'I can pick you up as if you were a cat and carry you there, or I can drag you to my study and if we are seen you will look most undignified. Take your choice, *mia amiga*. Do you come willingly, or do I use force? *Ay Dios mio!* One would think that I had the bedroom in mind. *Santina amada*, all I am proposing is that you come and be given a trinket. In fact, I have exactly in mind what will suit you! Come!'

Mutiny, and that strange feeling that she had water in the bones of her legs, made her drag behind him, and when his grip tightened on her wrist to the edge of pain, she gave a choked gasp. 'You're brutal!' she flung at him.

'Don't exaggerate,' he rejoined. 'That is the problem with very young women, they have this exasperating tendency to be melodramatic. With you I have not the slightest need to use brute force. You are so slight that Florentina has already suggested to me that you need fattening up. The good woman fears that I shall not have enough woman in my arms on my wedding night.'

'But we know differently, don't we?' Lise flung these words almost in his face as he very firmly pulled her into his study; the room which always seemed a little inquisitorial with its Cordoban leather walls and its massive desk and tall, hard-backed chairs.

'Yes.' He snapped the word at her, showing his teeth in a white biting way. His eyes raked her, and temper ran like a snarl between them. With his free hand he slammed the study door, and because the interior of the door was also lined with leather, Lise was suddenly framed against the dark red, a slim, pale-skinned figure in rose silk that was softly shaped to her slenderness. Her hair against the red leather took on a sudden startling fairness, and her grey eyes seemed darkened by the dark face looking down into them.

'You could go too far with me,' he said, and the words ran across her skin like a whiplash. 'Then you would know at last what it is like to be alone – entirely alone with a man. Be careful, angel hair, if you don't want defiance and threat to make a reality of my words.'

'I — I'd yell the place down,' she gasped, and she was almost unaware that she had drawn back close to the leather wall until she felt its cool touch against her bare arms. She shivered at the touch, and saw the lids narrow across Leandro's eyes.

'These walls are soundproof,' he drawled. 'That is the idea, that a man can work in peace, and also reprimand his staff without being overheard. Such walls would also make it possible for a man to do whatever he pleased with a woman, for her cries would not be heard. I could beat you, or make love to you, and our only witness would be that bronze figure on my desk.'

Lise stared at him, and so dark and menacing was his face in that moment that she knew with her every nerve that he was utterly capable of carrying out his threat. It wasn't only the castle that held echoes of the Moorish past; the old desires and inclinations still ran in the blood of this direct descendant of that long-dead lord of El Serafin; here in the courts and gardens lingered the tinkle of slave bracelets: there in Leandro's eyes smouldered the passion and the daring that would never die while he lived, and in his turn passed on the flame to his son.

The moment held such danger for Lise that she felt petrified. The slightest movement might trap her in his arms, for she knew instinctively that his cruelty was not of the kind that raised its hand against a woman. He had other ways . . . ways far more subtle . . . of inducing a woman to give in to him.

Lise dragged free of the magnetic glitter of his eyes, and she forced a shaky laugh to her lips. 'We're quarrelling like a couple of cats of different breeds,' she said. 'For no real reason, except that I seem to ruffle your fur, and you seem to ruffle mine. Let's stop it, please.'

'You don't like the fur to bristle?' Suddenly the very tip of his forefinger was against the skin of her arm, sliding down the soft crook of her elbow . . . and sending through her the most startling sensations. 'You are a smooth little cat, *amiga*. I am almost temped to find out if you purr.'

Then, with a mocking quirk of his black brow, he turned away from her and went to his desk. Lise could not relax, and could feel her legs trembling as she leaned there against the wall, and watched him open a drawer of that great carved Spanish desk and take from it a small flat case . . . of the sort in which jewellery was kept.

'Madrecita has already dropped the hint that I am being a little too ungenerous with the family jewels, and so a while ago I had a look in the safe to see if we had something that might tempt your saintly little soul. I am fully aware that you hate to wear the jewellery under false pretences, but it makes Madrecita happy, and if you were not such a little puritan it would make you happy, also. What is the matter? Do you feel that I am painting the artificial lily?'

'You are painting an artificial situation,' she said. 'Adding rock upon rock, so that when we finally need to escape, we'll find ourselves up to our necks.'

'You, at least, have a very pretty neck, *guapa*.' And so saying he came back to her, and something glittered in his fingers, so that they seemed alive with drops of blue and white fire. 'If you press any closer to that leather wall, my dear, you will leave your crucified impression. I really wonder which you hate the most, my touch, or my gifts.'

'I – I can return the gifts,' she said defiantly.

'Very true. So it is my touch which you dislike. Even soap, eh, cannot wash away a memory?' Now he was close again, and the gems sparkling in his fingers were diamonds, a necklace of them, to which was attached a heart made of a single sapphire. A dark blue sapphire, like the ring on her finger.

'Now like the family dentist I am going to say that you will hardly feel a thing,' he mocked. And locking his gaze with hers, he encircled her neck with the diamonds and fixed the clasp, and then quite deliberately he arranged the blue heart in the white hollow of her throat. 'There, child, it is all over. And not a mark on you.'

'There's no need to be so — so sarcastic,' she flared. 'I'm not a silly puritan, or some sort of saint, but I just don't like the way I've allowed myself to be entangled in your web of deceit. Decking me out in the family finery is bound to appeal to your mocking sense of humour, but I'm not amused.'

'No, my young Victorian, you would not be.' But this time when he spoke the mocking gleam was gone from his eyes and they held a brooding quality as they dwelt on her jewelled skin. 'All the same, the finery becomes you. There is fire and ice in diamonds, and in a girl not yet introduced to passion, and I have always considered that pearls are more suited to widows. That sapphire came into my family many years ago, by way of the Eastern line in our history and our veins. It is older than the ring, which was matched to it, but my mother never wore the heart. It had the kind of history she could not tolerate.'

'You mean that it was probably worn by a harem girl?' Lise could feel the weight of the heart-shaped sapphire against her throat, cool and smooth, and holding Leandro's gaze to her skin. A pulse in her throat beat quickly under the gem of glowing blue, and she wanted wildly to turn away from his eyes, so dark and disturbingly shaded by his thick lashes.

'Yes,' he drawled, 'a girl in scented silks, who bathed in a lotus pool, and wore stars of jasmine in her hair. But it isn't that aspect which you dislike, is it? Your sensitivity is of a different sort. You feel that only a false gem should represent our false relationship, eh?'

'I'm afraid I do,' she admitted. 'Wearing costume jewellery wouldn't trouble me in the least—'

'Then think of it as costume jewellery.'

'You know that's impossible, *señor*.' She drew a sigh. 'Having committed myself to your game of hearts, I have to play it your way, don't I?'

'At least with a dash of enjoyment,' he said quizzically. 'When you came in this afternoon in the company of Ana and Chano, you were looking eager and happy. Does my company cast such a cloud over you?'

'A small guilty cloud,' she admitted. 'The more I get to know the Condesa, the less do I like deceiving her. In fact—'

'Yes, Lise?' His tall figure seemed to tauten and to tower over her, so that in nervous reaction her fingers gripped the blue heart on its chain of small, perfect diamonds.

'I sometimes wonder if she suspects that we are playing a game. I have seen her look at me – strangely.'

'I have noticed that look also, and that is why I wish you to wear the necklace tonight. As I said before, Lise, it becomes you, and surely you have enough vanity to be pleased that you look most fair and appealing.' Abruptly he reached for her hand and carried it to his lips, and once again that tingling shock ran all down Lise's spine as she felt his lips press warm and hard against the inside of her wrist. It seemed that no matter how she fought this man, she remained as meshed in the personality of him as a moth caught in a web. With all her instincts she had to struggle, and yet with dominant ease he seemed always to subdue her.

'And now let us go to the *sala*,' he said, and with an air of true possession he tucked her hand into the crook of his arm. 'Everyone will be waiting for us.'

The evening meal was invariably served in a room adjoining the *sala*, a rather grand and solemn place in which to dine, with its long table set with heavy crystal and silver upon a cloth of wonderful Catalan lace, with the flames of candles standing still in the warm air this evening, the tawny candles grouped in the heavily sculptured candelabra that matched the rose bowls.

The food was always very Spanish, each course accompanied by a wine of the province. Lise never dared to take more than a few sips at each wine, for she had not the strong Latin head that had been trained from youth to accustom itself to the potency of these wines that were still made as in the old days, by being crushed by male dancers in great stone vats, after being collected from the vines by young girls who were still virgins. It seemed as if every potent factor of mountain life went into the wine; the sun, the wild breath of snow, the innocence and the knowledge.

The *sala* to which they returned at the end of the meal was a room looking on to the arcade of the courtyard where the passion vines and the bougainvillea splashed the walls and wafted their scents into the castle. These scents, mingling with the smoke of the cigars, created a dreamy atmosphere which Lise could not fight against. And this evening, to her astonished delight, gipsy dancers had been invited to come and entertain the Señor Conde and his family and guests.

The guitar music came with mysterious suddenness from where the fire-red blossoms hung the walls, and a voice began to sing to the music, and there came the click-click of castanets, like giant cicada wings, before the dancer actually appeared in the stream of light from the *sala*. She was tawny-skinned and supple, and she wore an ankle-length vermilion skirt in tiers of frills, with a full-sleeved blouse of white lace. Her hair gleamed dark like her eyes and was held by a high glittering comb, with a huge camellia nestling in its waves, and at either side of her face lay the traditional lovelocks, emphasizing the high thrust of her cheekbones.

The click of her finger-castanets and her high heels were almost hypnotic, and when the singing died away she began to dance with a lonely intensity that increasingly cried out for a partner. He came suddenly, slipping from the shadows like a shadow, and sleek as a panther he circled the girl, coming closer and closer to her until at last the frills of her red dress were sweeping against the black velvet of his tight-fitting pants. The pair of handsome creatures began to sway and mock each other with eyes and heels, and when he sank to one knee and showed his gleaming teeth, she whirled the frills of her scarlet dress right over his head, but when he leapt to his feet to claim her, she was out of his way again, and like two supple felines they mocked and dared each other to a fantastic array of dance steps, each step significant of the duel they were playing, one of passion and desire; of temper and torment; of chase and capture.

Lise sat entranced in the corner of a divan, for never before had she seen real *flamenco* dancing, or heard the music of it, a pulsing, tormenting, sensuous rhythm, beating its way into her body, and revealing to her the primitive urges that lay beneath the surface of clothing and skin.

She hadn't dreamed that Spanish dancing was so evocative, so that beauty and danger blended together into a flame of feeling and fire.

When fingers touched her shoulder, Lise almost cried out. 'It is only I.' The fingers tightened. 'You jumped like a cat just then. Do you like the *flamenco* dancing?'

'Marvellous!' she breathed. 'I had no idea it was so – so—'

'I am sure you didn't.' There was a deep amusement in

his voice. 'It is exciting, no?'

Unbearably exciting, she thought, and for a moment of exquisite torment she closed her eyes as those lean fingers brushed the nape of her neck and fondled the chain of diamonds. She wanted to beg him to leave her alone, to not play his game of make-believe so intimately. He knew that the Condesa had glanced their way; he meant his grandmother to suppose that the music and the dancing had aroused him to desire of his fair and innocent and altogether unlikely *novia*.

It was then, while the Spanish music played and echoed so evocatively along the arcade, that Lise came to realize the state that her emotions were getting into. She felt the swift stab of that realization; that silent crying out inside her that if only this were all real and not part of an elaborate pretence.

It was the pretence which she hated, not the man who touched her to make it look as if he wanted her.

Refreshments were taken out to the *flamenco* troupe, and when beckoned Lise went over to sit next to the Condesa, taking with her the coffee and *coñac* which had just been served. 'Well, my child,' a ringed hand touched her cheek, 'you are looking very pretty this evening, and I begin to feel convinced that you will be good for my good-looking devil of a grandson. I see he has given you the harem heart to wear, as my daughter-in-law used to call it. She was a sweet creature, but her passions were never as earthly as Latin passions usually are.'

'I understand that she is now a nun.' Lise took a long sip at her hot coffee enriched with brandy.

'Are you reminding me, child, that I speak of her as if she were no longer alive?' The Condesa gave Lise an old-fashioned look. 'I must admit that for a woman like myself a life of enclosed virtue strikes me as rather grim, but

Leandro's mother was always a creature more of the soul than the body, and for her the life is a satisfactory one. I hope, *pequeña*, that you are far less soulful? It would not do for my Leandro to take a woman to the altar who would not be prepared to enjoy the strong kisses of a strong man. He is a true son of the *sierras*, with the sun and the thunder in his blood. He is a grandson I am proud of and I want very much that he should be happy. I want this as much as I want his wife to make me a fine great-grandson.'

The Condesa moved her lace fan in deliberate little movements as she studied Lise, who hardly knew how she kept from jumping to her feet and dashing away from the disturbing aspects of this conversation. The fear and the confusion was there in her eyes, and abruptly the lace fan became very still.

'I hope,' said the Condesa freezingly, 'that you are not one of these ultra-modern girls who believes in putting a career before the production of a family? I hope, in fact, that you are not afraid of having babies for Leandro? You love him, eh?'

'Yes—' The word was spoken before Lise could withdraw it, or change it, or deny her own heart that spoke for her in that moment. *Yes*, she loved Leandro de Marcos Reyes as if he were the man she was to marry; as if he cared in return, instead of being in love with someone else, and being in a dilemma because that love would not be acceptable to this charming and proud old lady.

'Good, my child. Excellent!' The fan began to move again, and the rings to sparkle on the hands that were hungry to hold a child of Leandro's before their grip relaxed on life itself. 'It's love between two people that makes happy children. As a boy my Leandro was not always happy. He saw the lack of love between his parents; he heard the quarrels, and later on the rumours. The time has come for that *belo hombre* to be made happy.'

The Condesa turned her gaze to her grandson, who was at the other side of the *sala* talking to Chano and the young gipsy who had danced for them. He was taller than the other two men, his features hawk-like, and his stance, as he stood there with a glass of dark red wine in his hand, that of the man who owned all this and was aware of his authority without being too *arrogante* about it. Race and breeding marked him, and yet something of the Moor was there to be seen as his head was outlined against the arabesque of tiles ornamenting the arcade, the blue and silver weaving of colours, with a dash of scarlet.

Sudden emotion took hold of Lise, storming her heart and her body. She felt a devastating ardour, unwanted, unlooked for, but alive and strangely intoxicating, despite her knowledge of who it was he loved and desired.

'It pleases me that you love him,' said the Condesa, in a soft and meaningful voice. 'The other day I wondered – ah, but the elderly are always a little suspicious of the young, perhaps because as we grow older the memories of youth become suddenly sharper. In the middle years there is too much to do for a woman to have much time for remembering, but when the shadows start to grow long, then the memory becomes long again and one recalls the confusions of youth, the infatuations, and the doubts. Young women are rarely logical, for logic is a gift that comes with age. What are your doubts, *pequeña*? That life with a Spaniard will be a sort of tyranny?'

When Lise remained silent at the question, because it really was unanswerable, the Condesa gave a soft, slightly mocking laugh. 'He is a devil of a man, eh? But then you have certain advantages over the bolder type of woman he might well have brought here as his *novia*. The English girl blooms at nightfall, and the sensitive are always intensely in tune with nature. I am quite sure that there are times when you find Leandro overwhelming and utterly foreign, with sometimes in his mood the grumbling warmth of a thunderstorm. This is a very Latin characteristic and you must not be afraid of it, because there will be other times when he is all charm and will make sunlight in your heart. The sunlight will be worth the storm, eh?'

Oh yes, thought Lise. She had already guessed that Leandro de Marcos Reyes in love with a woman would be devastating in a number of ways, and that a woman would put up with his thunder to have him tender afterwards and smouldering with all that protective possessiveness of the Latin male.

'You are young and love frightens you a little,' murmured the Condesa, 'but that is how it should be – for a woman. It is this element which a man finds irresistible, and I am sure Leandro has sensed in you this retreat, and I know it pleases him because he has given you the sapphire to wear instead of the pearls which his mother preferred.'

And as the gipsy guitars began to play again, and as one of the moody yet exciting songs drifted in from the arcade where the passion vines clustered so thickly that they swept the ground, the Condesa told Lise the meaning of the words: ' "Love is like the olive tree, a mixture of silver and shadow, with its roots deep in the past and yet bearing fruit in the present. Love is the white dove, and the red ruby, and the wild sea lashing at the rocks on the shore. Love is tall as the palm, and low as the cushion, and among its tears are heard the singing birds.'

They were rather lovely words, so picturesque as to hold echoes of the Moorish past that lingered in these remote parts of Spain. As Lise relaxed among the divan cushions and listened to the song, her eyes brimmed with delight, and of all the memories she would carry away from the *castillo* she felt sure that the memory of tonight would be the most potent. The music, the dangerously soft dark eyes, the long gipsy hair held by silver combs.

It was a magical and lovely evening. Its enchantment could not be spoiled for her, not even by her knowledge that it must evolve as a memory and not as part of her future.

That night the Condesa was late going to her bedroom, and her grandson escorted her. Lise was in her own suite preparing for bed when there was a sudden tap upon her bedroom door, and thinking Ana had called for a chat, possibly about Chano, Lise pulled on her robe and went to open the door.

To her consternation Leandro stood there, and because he still wore his evening-suit he made her feel terribly undressed. She drew back at once from him, and instinctively she pulled together the gaping parts of her negligée over the chiffon of her nightdress ... chiffon for light travel and because it folded small in a suitcase, and not because she knew that it added a sort of glamour to a girl ready for bed, her face nude of make-up and her hair unloosed about her shoulders.

'W-what do you want?' The shock of seeing him at her bedroom door made her wide grey eyes look outraged; the truth was that her thoughts had been so full of him that she felt outraged by herself, as if she had secretly hoped to see him again tonight ... alone.

'Are you afraid that I want you?' he taunted, and with a hand negligently at rest in a pocket of his jacket he came into her room and closed the door with his other hand. Each of his movements seemed as deliberate as he could make them, yet there was a glint to his eyes that told Lise he had more purpose in coming here than to unnerve her with his presence.

He flicked his eyes over her face, and then gestured at the

velvet stool at the food of the bed. 'Please to sit down, Lise. I have something to discuss with you and it will be best if you are seated when I say what I have come to say.'

Lise now felt a new sort of alarm, and it tensed her, and made her speak with a pert defensiveness. 'I'd feel better if you sat down yourself, señor. When you stand towering over me I feel as if I'm facing the inquisitor. Please!' She gestured at one of the bedroom chairs, and was a little scared by a weakness in her legs as she sat down.

'Very well!' He sat down, and looked very dark against the grey silk brocade of the chair. Lise could not avoid his eyes and so she braved them, and wondered if their look of decision meant that he had decided to send her away.

'Chano brought me some letters from Madrid, one of which I did not wish to have sent by post to the castle in case a servant noticed the crest upon it and remarked on this to Manuela, who in turn might have informed Madrecita that I was in touch with her physician, not only one of the very best in Spain, but a man whose opinion I can trust to be the best available. But before we talk of that, I wish to know how much you like El Serafin. I really wish you could have been here in the springtime, when the mountains' lower slopes were wild with peonies, and the sun had a beneficent touch rather than a passionate one. Somehow you strike me as a springtime girl, young, tender, uncertain.'

He leaned forward and so held her gaze that she could not have looked away from him had she wished to do so. But she was intent on what he was saying, for she knew that he wasn't making casual conversation but was about to spring upon her something of deep concern to him. Something he had concealed behind an urbane manner all the evening, but was now about to reveal.

'You like El Serafin?' he pressed.

'How can I help but like it?' she parried.

'And you have grown to like the Condesa, eh?'

'Yes – but this gets more like an inquisitorial and I should like to know why.'

'I intend that you should know, but first tell me this, and don't think I ask it because I am a vain man, who considers himself irresistible to all women. Whenever I touch you, you withdraw as if I am about to bite you. Are you like this with all men, or just with me? Is there something about me – some foreign element which you find unattractive, or perhaps even alarming? Be frank, *señorita*.'

'In the circumstances, *señor*, it surely isn't relevant one way or the other.' As Lise spoke her fingers clenched the collar of her negligée as if to hide the pulse beating there, the throbbing giveaway of the state of her heart. Yes, he alarmed her, but not because she found him unattractive; seated there with that quizzical expression in his eyes, and with his black hair slightly rumpled on his brow, he was far more human and undemanding than she had yet known him, and she sensed that he was worried and wished to unburden himself. But did he feel that she would be unsympathetic if, as he supposed, she didn't like him?

'I have to tell you that it is relevant to the situation.' And all at once his face was sternly serious, so that tiny lines seemed to etch themselves more clearly at the outer corners of his eyes. 'I have this letter from Madrecita's physician which makes it plain that she would not survive a serious shock to her heart, and you know, as I most certainly know, that she has set her heart on seeing me married in the near future. She frets and grumbles and begs for this, and I have decided that if I don't give in to her on this issue she will fret herself into her grave. Her physician bears me out on this, and because I am in the fortunate position of being able to offer a woman a title, a castle, and a life that will not be hard, I am taking the bull by the horns and offering them to you, Lise. I am suggesting that we make our masquerade a reality; that you stay at El Serafin as my wife.'

His proposal was so astounding, so unexpected, that Lise was lost for words. She could only gaze at him in dumb-founded silence, though she felt sure that her heartbeats must be audible. He had to be joking. He couldn't mean what he had just said. *Wife*, to Leandro. *Wife unloved*, to the Conde de Marcos Reyes.

'Y-you can't be serious?'

'Indeed, and why not? Men are marrying every day of the week, so why not I? Why not you and I?'

'We aren't in love! You – you told me—'

'Yes, what did I tell you?' His voice had deepened in that dangerous way, as if daring her to say the words that were on the tip of her tongue.

'You implied, *señor*, that there was someone else, so I don't see how you can sit there and suggest that I – that we—'

'Would you find it too impossible to be my wife?' he broke in. 'You came to Spain seeking a fresh way of life, and to become actually part of Spanish life would surely be exciting for you. To all at El Serafin we are already at the threshold of marriage, so why not take the irrevocable step with me? Am I so impossible in your eyes as a husband?'

'You don't love me, Señor Conde, so I would soon become impossible in your eyes as a – a wife.' She flushed uncontrollably as she spoke the word, for it implied so many things – partner, comrade, mistress. 'You have told me how wretched was your mother's married life, because she knew herself to be part of an arrangement instead of a love match.'

'My mother, I came later to realize, was not a woman made for the earthly joys of loving.' Now his eyes were deliberately dominating Lise, forcing her to look at him, to listen, and so entice her into something that would be even more disastrous than their false engagement.

'Don't – please,' she begged. 'I – I won't listen to you!' And like a child afraid she threw her hands over her ears, and at once he came to his feet and bending over her forced her hands away from her ears, holding them firmly, with purpose, so that she was like a young supplicant there on the velvet bench in front of him.

'You are not at all like my mother,' he said, and each word had the incisive edge of sharp and cutting fact. 'I have watched, you about the castle, touching things and loving their tactile being, their history, and perhaps their strangeness. You seek contact with what is tangible, and only the other day I saw you bury your face in a sun-hot tangle of honeysuckle as if you would take the warmth and the scent into your very being. You are a sensuous young creature, Lise, though you might not be aware of the fact. My mother was a heavenly creature to look at, but men who looked at her made the mistake of thinking she wanted to touch or know earthly things. Each one of us, *pequeña*, is a victim of our own biology. The saintly woman can love everyone, provided there is a stone wall to protect her from being touched physically. You are not one of those, and I have been around long enough to know it. I could prove to you right now, *amiga*, that you are warm and giving in a very human way.'

And she, who had not been around but who was not altogether unworldly, knew at once what he meant. At once her hands tensed and twisted for freedom, and too late it was the wrong thing to do. He gave her one cynical look and the next instant jerked her to her feet and pulled her close and inescapably into his arms.

A pair of reactions jabbed instantaneously . . . as he pulled her to him the folds of her negligée opened and it was her chiffoned figure that was brought so painfully close to him. Secondly she was aware of the wild thrill that ran all through her body, the electrical response that took her breath and left her helplessly exposed to his lips as they came down hard on hers, while his arms found and held her in the chiffon, beneath which her slim body was bare, silky with youth and a love of bathing, and supple as the limb of a willow.

In some dim recess of her mind she had heard it said that some men could ravish with a kiss, and when his lips finally pulled free of hers and he looked down into her eyes, burning it seemed through the black shadows of his lashes, Lise felt as if she would never be wholly innocent again. As if he had plundered that, as well as her lips, leaving her scorched with a kind of shame because she had let him kiss her and had not raked his face with her fingernails or kicked his legs, or tried to save her feelings from that kiss which still throbbed on her mouth; from that touch which still sent painful little thrills from his fingertips to her very bones.

Her protest had to be made and with a painful wrenching movement away from him, she swung her hand and heard the sound of the slap before she felt the tingling sensation in her fingers and realized that she had hit him across the face.

She wasn't sorry, she was glad. It had probably never happened to him before, and would show him that she wasn't a girl to be treated as if she were some light creature, accustomed to being kissed in that fierce and foreign way.

Her grey eyes blazed as she watched him thrust the black hair from his brow, and with a sardonic quirk of his eyebrow touch his cheek. 'I knew there was fire in you, and that you weren't a little piece of ice,' he drawled. 'Contrary to what you may think at this moment, I am not made angry by your reaction, but I am more than ever certain that a marriage between us would not be altogether a misalliance. It could have rewarding aspects to it, for both of us, for I am not advocating one of those arid relationships in which the husband and wife politely agree to appear married without ever being more than guardian and ward. I should want a wife, for my own sake, and for the sake of the great-grandchild the Condesa will cling to life to see, if I marry quite soon.'

'And what of the woman – the woman you really love?' Lise had to ask, had to end this madness before she became as mad as he and agreed to his reckless proposal. 'Are you going to give up all you really want – in this Quixotic way? Do you really expect me to agree to such a – a marriage, when I know that I am just a means to provide you and the Condesa with that – that precious future link. What do you take me for, Señor Conde? Do you truly think I could marry a man for material things alone? I'd need to be wildly in love—'

'Then, *pequeña*, it will be my task to make you love me, won't it? As for other women, they will have to be disregarded.'

'As easily as that?' she asked, scornfully. 'Love doesn't seem to mean very much to you, *señor*? I gather that with you it is just a physical thing, in which the heart can be switched on and off, to provide heat or coolness to suit your mood of the moment. That may be the Latin way, but I am English—'

'I am very aware that you are English.' His eyes flashed over her, and amusement of a wicked sort leapt into them as she dragged together the folds of her robe. 'And that is why I am going to give you a little time to think over my proposal. A little time, *señorita*, but not too much, so that Madrecita worries and frets too much.'

'I realize your dilemma with regard to the Condesa,' said Lise, a shaken note in her voice. 'I do see that it would be difficult for you to introduce to her a woman who has been divorced – but it isn't fair of you to expect me to fill the breach. I won't give in to you—'

'We will see.' His lips quirked and he fingered his jaw again. 'I like your fighting spirit, Lise – among other things.' And with a slightly mocking bow he turned and walked to the door, tall, lithe and accustomed to having his own way. Lise couldn't see him go without a last fling of defiance.

'I shall find some way to get away from your castle, *señor*. I'm not a prisoner here!'

He turned briefly to look at her, and seeing his face again, and that tiny smile that glimmered in his eyes, was enough to make her heart lurch. And when the door closed behind him she knew how empty were her defiant words. She was his prisoner . . . his because her wildly beating heart told her so.

CHAPTER SEVEN

It seemed to Lise that she lay awake far into the night, and when at last she slept, she fell so soundly asleep that she awoke to find the sun flooding so warm into her room that she knew at once that the morning was well advanced.

She rose and bathed and dressed in a sleeveless blouse with her tangerine slacks. She went downstairs in search of Ana and Chano, and learned that they had gone out early in his car and had taken a picnic lunch with them. Lise didn't begrudge them their desire to be alone together, but it left her alone at the castle to face the master of it and to be reminded again of his fantastic proposal of the night before; and of his kiss that to him had been an experiment, a way of proving that he could make her respond to him, and give in to him.

Lise drank coffee at a table on the patio and stormily told herself that she was not going to give in so easily. She would find out if her car was in order and get away from him as soon as possible. Playing his fiancée had held danger enough, but this new plan of his, that they become truly engaged, held deeps from which she must draw back before she fell headlong into them.

She poured herself another cup of coffee, but just couldn't face the food under the silver covers.

The sun lay warm over the tiles of the patio, and over the flowering plants whose scents in daylight were less sensuous than they had been last night, while the gipsy music had played, and this impossible plan of the Conde's had crystallized in his mind. It was all in his mind, because what heart he had was shared between his grandmother and that glamorous woman in Madrid. He had no heart to give to herself and he supposed that it was enough that he offered his castle and his name.

And after that, if Lise had been crazy enough to agree to become his wife of convenience, would he then have made Franquista his mistress, just as his father had made another woman more important to him than his wife? Franquista was worldly, and it might suit her to be the fashionable mistress rather than the wife at El Serafin, which was miles from the distractions of city life, and where the people were rather old-fashioned and expected a certain decorum from the mistress of the *castillo*.

Yes, viewed dispassionately, the new turn of events would seem to suit Leandro admirably. His grandmother was saved from the real truth, and he had the best of two worlds, the quiet one here in the mountains, and the gay one in Madrid, where his business was and where he would no doubt reside for most of the time.

Lise rose to her feet and took a restless ramble about the patio. He had not even suggested that the marriage be one in name only; he had told her quite frankly that she would be expected to respond to him and in due course bear him this child which his *madrecita* wanted so much.

She had paused in front of a sprawling bush of camellias, and the rich white beauty of them made her think of weddings, and all the intimacy that was entailed in becoming the wife of a man. And a man such as Leandro, who was Latin to his very bones, would demand love of any woman who was intimately involved with him. He did not know, must not know, that Lise had already fallen victim to his fascination. If he learned that she felt herself on the verge of falling madly in love with him, then he would make it impossible for her to leave. He was experienced, he knew women, and he would know all too well how to kindle her emotions until she wanted only one thing in life . . . him.

Right now . . . oh, right this minute she had to find some small escape, where away from the fascinating environs of the castle she could plan more carefully her escape from Leandro and the forceful way he was invading her heart, her very life.

She would go to the beach! She had a bathing-suit in her room, and if she hurried she would be out of the castle within ten minutes, with no chance of being caught by Leandro, who at any moment might be riding back from his inspection of the olive plantation, or the one or two houses that needed some repairs. She had noticed that while here at El Serafin he was rarely relaxed, and she was inclined to wonder if it was because he missed the company of Franquista.

Lise gnawed her lip as she ran up the stairs to fetch her beach things. If he missed Franquista now, whatever would he be like with a young, untried wife on his hands; someone whom he married because her innocence pleased his grandmother, and who was youthful and healthy enough to give him a fine son?

She was at the mirror, bunching the fair hair at the crown of her head, when she saw the colour storm into her cheeks, and imagined for possibly the first time in her life (up until now her image of love had been purely dreamlike) what it would be like to have a man such as Leandro taking her to himself in a passion that would not stop at long, demanding kisses. She had heard that women had to be in love in order to enjoy passion, but she knew enough – perhaps from that kiss last night – to realize that men were different. She had felt the pleasure which Leandro had drawn from that kiss, and she had felt the intake of his breath when his hands had found her so slim and smooth under the chiffon of her night-dress. She knew that he could take her without love. . . but she couldn't face the thought of being no more than an appeasement for his love of someone else. An hour's passion to cool ardour, and to provide the next heir to the Marcos Reyes title and estate.

Lise snatched her bathing-suit from the drawer, grabbed a large Turkish towel from the bathroom, and fled from the room which reminded her too vividly of those entirely physical moments last night in the arms of Leandro.

Maids were at work in the bedrooms, and she caught a glimpse of Manuela as she hastened toward the stairs. She pretended to be lost in thought, and upon reaching the hall she took to her heels and ran, the suit and towel clutched in her hand, heading through the grounds of the castle in the direction of the far-down gleam of blue water dotted by black rocks.

The steps that led down to the beach had been hacked out of the cliffside and there seemed to be hundreds of them, for the castle was perched high above the sea so that the Marcos Reyes might have this marvellous view and their privacy. As Lise neared the beach she was glad to see that she would have it to herself. She felt as if she had never needed so much to be alone, and there was a certain comfort in the sound of bird calls and the roll of the water, lapping and hissing when it reached the rocks.

Lise ran behind a high dry rock and quickly shed her dress and her underclothes. She stepped into her bathing-suit and quickly pulled the straps over her shoulders, and kicking off her sandals she made for the water, feeling the sand like hot velvet under her bare feet. She felt eagerly certain that the water would be warm when she entered it, but she found to her surprise that it was quite cool, and she kicked out energetically in order to keep warm and to get used to the coolness as soon as possible.

Having been brought up by a brother she had been introduced at an early age to the pleasures and dangers of swimming, and this morning she felt a little reckless, as if she must swim until she exhausted herself and her troubled thoughts lost their clarity and everything became hazy and less sharply defined.

Though cool the water was silky and buoyant, and setting as her target a larger thrust of rock far out in the blue she swam steadily and with purpose, as if racing an invisible opponent. When she reached the rock, which was larger than she had supposed, she hauled herself on to it and took deep breaths of the tangy, refreshing air. Gazing back across the sea she realized that she had covered about a mile, for the *castillo* seemed etched like a fabled toy against the sky and the peaks, and as she stared at it, so beautiful and unreal in the distance, she tried to imagine what it would be like to become part of such a place.

She, Lise Harding, in residence there as the mistress, the person who gave the household orders, and who received the Conde's guests, and learned all the intricate secrets of being wife to Leandro.

No, it was all as unreal as the castle looked in the distance. It was a mirage that could not be grasped, and the only reality was that Leandro did not love her. And without his love, she told herself, she couldn't face all the rest.

Suddenly she shivered, for the wind on her wet body was almost cold, and she plunged back into the water and headed in the direction of the beach.

She was about halfway there when the sudden pain of cramp gripped her left leg and held it for a frightening moment in a vice from which it couldn't move. She floundered in the water and had breathed the salty moisture before she could stop herself and next moment was gasping and choking and struggling to move the limb that had contracted itself into such a cramped position that the slightest effort to straighten the leg caused such agony that her head reeled and all the rules about this sort of thing seemed to explode into panic. A choked scream broke from her, and though her struggles only increased her intake of water and her pain, she couldn't seem to control her frightened body. She knew . . . despairingly she knew that she was going to drown, far out from the safety of the beach, here in the waters of a foreign bay, and as the nightmare gripped her, as the vice of cramp gripped her leg muscles, she cried out again and her pounding brain that was going dark knew the name that she cried as she gagged against the salty sea in her throat and felt as if some other nameless thing were dragging her under, completely under the cold weight of the water, digging its invisible claws in the calf of her leg.

Suddenly the claws seemed to have hold of her upper body, and she fought like a mad thing, hearing words she couldn't grasp with her spinning mind, and then stunned right out of her mind as a fist clipped itself against her jaw and she went still, senseless, painless . . . and didn't waken again until there was the crushy warmth of sand under her body, and the burning tang of something against her lips. As she protested her eyes opened and a dark face came into focus above her and she became aware that a finger was stroking her lips with brandy, bringing back the life to them, so that instinctively her tongue sought that warm source of life.

'You like that, eh? You are alive again now the sea water has expelled itself.'

She stared up at him, limp as a wrung-out rag, and so exhausted that she could only plead with her eyes for an actual swallow of the brandy.

Leandro lifted her against his arm and put the lip of the flask to her lips. She swallowed and felt the harshness of her throat, and realized what he had meant about the sea water being expelled from her. She must have gulped quite a lot of it, and he, presumably, had pumped it out of her with those hands she had fought so crazily, out there in the sea.

Again with her eyes alone she questioned him, and she saw a twist to his lips, and felt him touch her aching jaw. 'I saw you going down the beach steps as I was riding back from the plantation, and I noticed you had a bathing-suit with you. It was fortuitous that I decided to take a swim myself – tell me, do you often get leg cramp in that way? When you started to struggle I guessed it was that. There are no sharks in our bay, for the water is too cool for them, but when I reached you and you increased your struggles, I am sure that you thought I was a shark – the tiger variety, eh?' With an angry sort of solicitude he brushed the wet hair from her brow. 'About the leg cramp – has it ever happened like that before?'

She shook her head. 'Never.' Her voice was still husky, still shaken. 'I–I think I must have got cold when I swam out to that large rock in the bay. I probably lost track of time while I rested there, and on the way back the cold got to my leg. It was – awful. I really believed my number was up. You – you hit me!' As the realization struck at her, she looked at him with shocked eyes.

'You were fighting me so much that I had to, *pequeña*. Do you now feel a little better – well enough for me to take you back to the castle?'

'I–I think so.' She forced herself to sit up, and then as everything seemed to go spinning round in her head, she clutched at his bare shoulder, and then leaned weakly against him. 'Let me stay a while longer—'

'No, you will catch cold. I have dried you as much as possible, but you need a hot bath, and a few hours' rest in your bed.' As he spoke he stood up and raised her to her feet, and then next moment she found herself lifted into his arms, with her arms instinctively seeking a hold around his neck.

'Y-you aren't going to carry me?' She thought of all those steps. 'Leandro, you can't! If you'll only wait, my strength will be back and I shall manage all right.'

'There is another way under the cliffs, a path to the cellars which was used, as you can probably guess, for other purposes in days gone by. Sad to say, Spanish brandy is not as good as the French sort, and I had an ancestor who enjoyed a tot of brandy almost as much as he enjoyed the smuggling. Come! This is the way we go.'

'My clothes,' she cried out. 'I left them behind a rock.'

'Someone will be sent to fetch them.' His sandalled feet ploughed through the sand and they passed the cliff steps and he made for a moon-shaped scoop in the cliffs, with some tall rocks guarding the entrance. He entered the cave, which seemed suddenly dark to Lise, who clung to his shoulders and felt the smooth heat of them as he carried her for several yards into the dimness. There in the dimness, and despite her feeling of weakness, she felt a sudden strange elation, which she supposed was due to her recent fright and recovery, and finding it was Leandro who had come to her rescue. Also there was a kind of crazy adventure feeling about being alone with him in a smugglers' cave, which he seemed to know well, probably from his youth, for he soon located the creaking old door that led into the cellars, where he pulled a cord and a light came on.

She saw at once that they were surrounded by wooden racks of long-necked wine bottles, and against the rough, dirty-white walls stood old casks bound in copper, and from the dark old beams hung dusty cobwebs, and something scuttled in a corner.

It was the kind of place to hold boyhood memories of pirate games and being shipwrecked, and when Lise glanced

up at him and saw his lip quirk she knew that he was remembering those far-off days when he had probably sensed
that his parents were not happy together and had found here
a place of escape.

'How are you feeling now?' He paused beneath the light
of the bare hanging bulb and studied her face. 'You are still
pale, but your breathing seems easier.'

'I'm much better, *señor*, thank you. I could walk—'

'No, we have only to traverse a passageway and some
steps and to your surprise, and perhaps your relief, you will
find yourself in the hall of the castle.'

'There are so many steps to the beach, *señor*.' Despite
last night, and despite his rescue of her this morning, she felt
a choking sense of shyness and couldn't bring herself to say
his name. She felt the slightly mocking glance which he gave
her as they continued on their way along the vaulted passage, which felt chilly, and which perhaps was why he drew
her closer to his chest, which was warm and rough with
dark hair, in which was meshed a Latin medal with a glint
of gold to it.

'That is because you approach them through the gardens,
señorita, which elevate by the gradual use of steps in orna-
mental pairs and hardly noticed because of the foliage and the
flowers. We are proud of the castle gardens, in which are
planted shrubs and blooms from all parts of the world,
wherever a Marcos Reyes has travelled. I brought red roses
from England when I was there, and some white hy-
drangeas. Did you not notice?'

'Well, I was in rather a hurry—'

'And why? What made you hurry so? Were you afraid of
seeing me?'

'Perhaps,' she admitted, and was glad when they stepped
into the hall of the castle, which had more familiarity and
less intimacy than the dimness of the cellars. '*Señor*, I can

manage now, if you will let me go.'

'It is not my intention to let you go.' Words which Lise felt sure had a double meaning as he carried her across the hall and all the way up to her room, where at last he set her upon her feet.

'For once a Spaniard is grateful that a girl is not plump,' he said dryly. 'Now I shall send a girl to you and she will run you a hot bath and see to it that you rest in bed for a while—'

'*Señor*,' she caught at his arm, 'I can do those things for myself, so please don't send anyone. I'm not helpless.'

'A while ago you were.' His fingers caught at her chin and for a long moment he forced her to look at him. 'You must not be so independent, *amiga*. Here in Spain we help each other and don't rush by because it might be too much trouble or cause a bother for us. I will leave you alone if you make me the promise that you will soak in a hot bath and then try to sleep and forget your alarming experience.'

'I promise.' Then, shakily, she added her grateful thanks that he had saved her life.

'It was fortunate that I saw you heading for the beach.' He frowned at her. 'Next time you wish to go swimming, you will ask for my company or that of Ana. I suppose you took it for granted the water would be warm? Alas, this isn't so. In this part of the coast the depths are extreme and can be very dangerous, as you learned today. Now hurry to your bath. *Até a vista.*'

He turned on his heel and was gone, and Lise was glad to obey his orders with regard to running a bath and taking a long, drowsy soak. She was seated on the side of her bed, towelling her damp hair, when fingers tapped her door and it opened to admit one of the young maids, who carried a small round tray on which glinted a silver cup.

'The Señor Conde says that you had a little trouble at the

beach and I am to bring you this, *señorita*.' The girl placed the cup in Lise's hand, and at once she caught the aroma of mixed herbs and a strong dash of spirit and hot lemonade. When she tasted the toddy she caught the taste of honey as well. 'It's delicious!' she gasped.

'*Si, señorita*.' The young maid broke into a smile as she surveyed the master's *novia*, who with her hair all tousled about her face, and wearing her camel dressing gown, looked far from capable of ever handling an important Spaniard and his establishment. 'It is a special remedy of the Doña Manuela's.'

'Oh, does she know about me?' Lise was instantly anxious. 'I do hope she won't go telling the Condesa. I'm all right now and I don't want her to be worried.'

'I am sure the Señor Conde would not permit that she be worried, *señorita*.' The maid took the empty cup and turned back the bedclothes. 'I will tuck you in, and then draw the curtains to keep out the sun. *Si*, that is good? The pillows are just right?'

'Perfect, thank you.' Already Lise's eyelids were growing heavy and a moment before she slipped into sleep she guessed that something in the toddy had produced this lovely lethargy; this relaxation of her body and her nerves. On her lips lingered the sweetness of honey and lemon, and gone was the salty taste of the sea. Gone was that nightmare certainty that she was about to drown in the grip of the sea. Leandro had pulled her free of that grip . . . into his own arms that had felt so warm . . . so hard to resist.

In the next few days it came as a relief to Lise never to find herself entirely alone with Leandro. Details of her mishap had not reached the ears of the Condesa, otherwise she would have mentioned it, and Lise felt very grateful for the discretion of Manuela, one of those good-natured people who hover on the fringes of other people's love affairs and dramas without ever becoming involved in one of her own. Ana did say that as a younger woman Manuela had been fond of a man, but he had been poor and had gone off to Mexico to make his fortune, and by the time it had been made Manuela had become too attached to the Condesa to ever leave her. She seemed happy enough, but Lise found herself wondering these days if any woman could be truly happy without a man to love her.

This was a train of thought which had merely flashed through Lise's mind in what now seemed those far-off days in London, where the sanity of work had held sway over her instead of the combined fascination of a castle and its master.

Yes, it had to be admitted that he fascinated her, and since he had saved her life she felt a new and reluctant warmth towards him. She supposed that he had become a sort of hero in her eyes, but none the more for that she wasn't – she forcibly told herself – going to be coerced into a marriage that on his side would be a mere matter of expediency; a fairly easy way of satisfying duty without giving up his associations in Madrid.

How convenient for him! A young wife tucked away at El Serafin, whom he would no doubt ensure was speedily provided with a child, while he continued to enjoy the gay and exciting company of the woman he truly preferred.

Lise was moodily lost in her thoughts when footsteps sounded on the tiles leading to the bougainvillea arbour, and Lise, whose senses as well as her ears recognized the length of the stride, shrank back among the purple and white flowers in the hope that he would pass by and not see her.

It was a forlorn hope, for she was wearing the tangerine slacks that gave her away and his quick eye caught the flash of bright colour and he came to a halt in the entrance of the arbour, completely blocking it so there was no escape from him. 'Ah, there you are! I have been searching for you, and find you in hiding.' His eyes glinted under the black sweep of hair as he stood regarding her, hands thrust into the pockets of his dark blue trousers, with which he wore a matching silk shirt open across the dark brown throat.

His look of vigour was so stunning that Lise caught her breath, framed herself against the lushest bloom of the tropics, planted long ago, she had learned, by a Marcos Reyes who had been for a time the Governor of a Caribbean island. The history and drama of this family was enough to go to a girl's head without the addition of a man who looked so darkly handsome and unconquerable as he stood there. Even the beautiful Franquista had not conquered him to the extent where he would ignore duty to his family name and risk striking the Condesa a mortal blow. Even she was a mere woman to be left waiting while he settled his domestic affairs. Even she, that magnetic woman with the full figure and the raven hair beloved of the Spaniard.

Casually, with his gaze still upon her, the Conde took a cheroot case from a hip pocket and also a lighter. With deliberate movements of his lean hands he extracted one of the dark cheroots and inserted it between his lips. Then he flicked on the lighter and carried the small flame to the tip, which swiftly smouldered. He then rested a shoulder against the arching trelliswork, and the smoke of his cheroot mingled with the tang of the flowers.

'There is to be no more evasion of the matter I mentioned the other day,' he said crisply. 'Hiding yourself away from me won't induce me to forget that I asked you to be my wife. I now require an answer, and what more romantic surroundings than these? Around us the bougainvillea and across the patio the cool sound of water in the basins of the fountain.'

Again his left hand carried the cheroot to his lips, and her gaze followed the movement as if magnified, for there was something extraordinarily sensuous in the way a Spaniard smoked . . . in fact, everything about this particular Spaniard was sensuous; his glance, his mouth, and his male grace of body.

'You particularly like this part of the garden, don't you?' The aromatic smoke drifted from the proud arch of his nostrils. 'That mauve-starred love-vine over there, draping Pan, the god of mischief. The rich scent of the juniper trees, and the bird-pepper trees hanging their flame fruits above the patio walls, with those small stone towers at the corners. Just think to yourself that one simple word can make it yours. This and all the rest.'

'And you!' She broke in on his seducing speech. 'You above all, *señor*, and you would make sure I never forgot it. I'd have to pay—'

'In what coin exactly!' Suddenly his eyes held that dangerous promise of an unpredictable move. 'If we are making out accounts, then let us be clear about them. You say you would have to pay, which I take to mean with your loyalty and your person. Am I correct?'

'Yes.' She flushed slightly. 'You might marry without love, but you would make darned sure of the woman. She'd have to do her duty by you, and if she ever blemished your name, I feel pretty sure you'd break her neck, and with so many steps about the place you could always make it look as if she tripped and fell.'

'So you consider me ruthless, eh? You truly believe that I would be capable of the old ways of Spain and would treat a straying wife in a savage way?' As smoke wreathed itself about his features, he lounged there with a trail of purple flowers against his shoulder and he gravely considered her judgment of him. Finally he inclined his dark head and a little flame of wickedness kindled in his eyes. Those eyes wandered over her, as if already he was picturing her in the role of his wife and his possession. There was no other way to consider a wife in connection with him; Lise felt sure of that.

'So you judge me the perfect example of Spanish cruelty, eh? With, perhaps, a little courtesy thrown in; the velvet glove hiding the iron hand.' He laughed in his soft and mocking way. 'So that is why you hesitate to marry me. You think you might stray and I might break your slim white neck.'

'Wouldn't you?' The words flung themselves from her lips.

'Of course,' he said smoothly. 'I am glad you are perceptive enough to judge my character, for it never does for a woman to go into marriage with a blindfold over her eyes. Or for that matter to be so desperately in love with a man that she would care for nothing, except to be with him. Neither way is your way, is it, Lise? I am glad of that, as basically this is an arrangement rather than a—'

'But I haven't said I'll marry you,' Lise broke in, and her heart thumped at the words. 'I haven't committed myself to your proposal, and I have no intention of doing so—'

'Have you not?' Even as he spoke he dropped the end of his cheroot to the ground and took a step into the arbour, and then another, until Lise was pressing herself bodily against the bougainvillea. 'There is no need for you to take such a defensive attitude, my dear. But it is an attitude which makes me curious – I wonder what you fear the most, my kisses or my temper?'

'Don't you dare to touch me!' Her hands clenched the purple and white flowers that clustered all about her, as if she could pull them around her like a shield. But they were as fragile in her hands as she would be in his and she felt the petals falling apart as she gripped them, and she was shocked by her own violence, her own panicky vandalism, and by the Victorian appeal which leapt to her lips. It did not surprise her to see his lips quirk in derision as he stood over her ... Don Dark Angel ... devil and saviour ... for she would not be here to defy him if he hadn't pulled her out of the sea.

'Do I now have to repay you for the other day?' she demanded. 'I guessed it would come to this, as you spoke just now about making up accounts.'

'Why not?' he drawled. 'You do owe me something, and as I must find a suitable wife it seems pointless to go searching beyond this point, doesn't it?'

'There is Ana – she is a Latin girl and was prepared before I came to – to accept a proposal from you, should you make one. The Condesa loves her—'

'And so does Chano,' he broke in, and he loomed so close to Lise that she could see the saintly profile on the medal in the opening of his shirt, dark blue and silky against his brown and supple skin. She could see the crisp curl of the hairs on his chest, and breathe on him the tang of the soap with which he had scrubbed himself. Oh God, she knew he was ruthless and yet she could feel her senses being swayed by his male vigour. She knew he was the lover of another woman, yet right now he was far from that woman and too close to Lise for her heart to be in control of itself. She could feel her heart dipping, and then rising into her throat, as if she were on some emotional roller-coaster that was both thrilling and fearful.

Her pulses were in a riot, and her nerves were tingling, for she knew he meant to take hold of her and there was no way of escape, not here where the bougainvillea grew so thick and close that she was trapped in it as his hands reached for her and swung her close against his hard warmth of body and limb, and secret heart.

'Never dare a Spaniard,' he said mockingly, 'for he is the man who dares the sharp-horned bull . . . and you, *pequeña*, have a much softer hide, even if you have the obstinate spirit.' He bent his head and laid a warm-lipped kiss against her cheek, and then as his lips lingered there and she felt all the potent danger in his lithe body, the old panic whipped at her and made her jerk her face away from him. She knew immediately that she had done the wrong thing, for it was in his nature to enjoy conflict rather than compliance, and if she had submitted tamely to his kiss he would have released her instead of tightening his arms about her.

'Come, it's time you learned how to react to a man like a woman instead of a nervous child. Put your arms about my neck! *Al momento!*'

'Don't give me orders!' She threshed in his arms for escape, and her struggles only seemed to bring her closer to him; closer still to the knowledge that she didn't really wish to fight him. As all these new and unwanted emotions erupted within her, making her hate herself for wanting him, she drove that self-hate into him, like the point of a knife.

'I don't react like a nervous child,' she stormed. 'I merely react like a woman who can't endure to be touched by some other woman's lover. What do you take me for! Do you think I'm so hard up that I'll take you on regardless of what I know?' As her grey eyes blazed defiance at him, and as she saw the glittering fury come alive in his eyes, the arbour in which they stood lost its romantic aura and became a cage in which a pair of felines prepared to claw and snarl. Already his fingers were bruising her when very clearly there came the sound of a stick on the flagstones beyond the arbour, and Lise saw the rapid change in Leandro's expression a moment before the figure of his grandmother appeared beyond his shoulder, pausing at the entrance to the arbour, with Manuela in attendance.

Though Leandro could not see his grandmother, Lise knew that he had recognized the sound of her stick, which she always used when taking a short walk in the sunshine of the gardens. Even as Lise saw the Condesa, Leandro swiftly bent his head to hide the look in Lise's eyes and the next instant his lips were against hers, ordering her in a fierce whisper to put her arms about him.

She obeyed him in a blind way, and then her traitor body was yielding to the demand of his arms, to the pressure of his mouth, and through the tumult of his kiss she knew that his grandmother watched them, and it wasn't until there came the receding sound of her stick, and the murmur of her voice, that Leandro drew his mouth from Lise's forcibly kissed lips.

A violence that from the doorway of the arbor would have taken on the look of mutual passion, there in the purple shadow of the bougainvillea.

Lise's bare arms slid from his shoulders, but a moment longer his arms remained about her slim body. 'I could not allow Madrecita to see us fighting,' he said, in clipped tones. 'It would have upset her and she has not the resilience of youth to bounce back from a shock. She will now assume the obvious, that we are finding it difficult to stay apart from each other. Lise, would you find it so impossible to become a Marcos Reyes? Could you not learn to tolerate my Spanish pride – and passion?'

'You – you and the Condesa between you seem to be leaving me with little choice in the matter.' Lise had never felt so unsure of herself and so shaken by another human being. If only he cared . . . if only there was more on his side than a sense of duty and honour. If only there had been love in his kiss instead of angry passion . . . anger against the circumstances that drove him to take a wife to suit his grandmother . . . and passion aroused because he was very much a man and a long way from the embrace of that other woman.

'Both of you – you make me feel as if I owe you myself,' she went on shakily. 'If I went away now I'd feel as if I were dealing the Condesa her death blow . . . and if you had not been around the other day I'd have died. It's all so – so inexorable, as if I no longer have any say in my own future.'

'Does a future at El Serafin seem so intolerable?' He spoke with the old bite of mockery in his voice, and as he drew his hands from her waist he allowed his fingers to press, almost to caress her. She shivered and could not stop herself, and at once his hands withdrew and he must have thought that she shivered with dislike of his touch, for there was a certain savagery in the way he thrust those hands into the pocket of his trousers.

'Yes,' he said crisply, 'the dilemma is now yours as well as mine. I had to kiss you to stop you from saying something to me that would have hurt and shocked Madrecita. I had to make it look as if we came here to the arbour to make love, and now she has witnessed that embrace she will naturally assume that we are in love. If she were your grandmother, old and tired and clinging to the hope of another generation of her blood and bone, could you wilfully hurt her?'

'I – I shouldn't do it wilfully,' Lise protested.

'Why do it at all?' he asked, and he was watching her with narrowed eyes, their darkness fixed upon the paleness of her face . . . pale but for the hurtful bloom his lips had brought to her lips. 'There is no young man in England to whom you wish to return, otherwise you would not have come to Spain alone, searching for a job. You are free to choose.'

'But you are not – not really,' she cried out. 'You do have someone to whom you wish to return.'

'That is beside the point—'

'I think it's very much to the point.' Lise tilted her chin and drew herself up very straight. 'I don't fancy taking second place in the life of the man I marry. I happen to believe in love and the sanctity of marriage, and I'm afraid it wouldn't suit me to be aware all the time of my husband's mistress in Madrid. I'd hate that, *señor*, as much as you would hate me if I ever sullied the Marcos Reyes name with another man.'

'I see.' For a long moment he lounged against the wall of the arbour, and everything was silent but for the buzzing of a bee somewhere in the heart of a flower. It was somehow a symbolic sound, for Lise felt as if her own heart was being plundered by the invasive love it neither sought nor welcomed. Her entire being felt at the mercy of Leandro's gaze, as if he could penetrate her body with his eyes alone and see how wildly her heart was beating.

'So, Lise, you think I would treat my wife as my father treated my mother?'

'We all inherit traits from our parents, don't we?' It took nerve to meet his eyes so steadily; it took hope that her own eyes did not reveal the devastation he had wrought with her feelings. 'It might be in the Latin temperament to enjoy being martyred, but I don't fancy the procedure myself.'

'Martyred?' The word came flickering through the air like the very tip of a lash. 'Is that how you think of marriage with a Marcos Reyes?'

'Yes.' The word dropped into the silence like silk into flame; like a stone hitting glass. It had the sting of truth. 'Yes, *señor*, I'm afraid I do.'

'Afraid?' he murmured, and he gave her the strangest smile, but behind that smile lay a glitter of fury, and Lise saw it and she wanted to be gone from this arbour and out of his reach, for she knew she had truly angered him and deep in her heart lay the wish that it could have been otherwise. It would have been so much easier on the nerves and the emotions to have given in to him, but she couldn't endure the knowledge that he wanted only to make use of her.

'May I go now?' she asked stiffly. 'I promised to cut out a dress for Ana and she'll be wondering what has become of me.'

'Before you go,' he gritted, 'you had better be warned that Madrecita is not yet ready for your kind of impetuous truth. We will continue as we are – do you understand me? If it isn't too much of a martyrdom.'

'I don't think you'd care even if it was,' she rejoined. 'I–I have no wilful wish to hurt the Condesa, but you must find some way to let me off this hook. I have my own life to live. My own way to go. I know you saved my life and I'm terribly grateful, but that doesn't mean that I have to sacrifice myself—'

'Enough!' This time the sharp lash of his tone made her flinch. 'You have really said more than enough.' And as he spoke he moved aside from the entrance and his arm swept the bougainvillea. At once a large bee flew out from the flowers, disturbed and making a loud buzzing sound. In its anger it seemed to make a beeline for the nearest object, and Lise gave a smothered cry as it struck at the Conde's face and then flew swiftly out of the arbour.

'*Mierda!*' He flung up a hand and Lise saw with alarm that the great bee had stung Leandro close to the left eye. '*Dios*, that felt like a hot needle!'

'You must have it seen to, at once!' Lise was by his side, and anxiety wiped other things from her mind for the moment. '*Señor*, the sting is close to your eye and a doctor should attend to it.'

'Anxious – for me?' He peered down at her in a sardonic way. 'You are right about the eye, of course, so will you be so good as to run indoors and telephone the doctor? You will see the number there on the telephone pad, with the doctor's name – *espere un momento*!' As she was about to dart away. 'You will ensure that Madrecita hears nothing of your call.'

'Of course, *señor*.' Lise ran swiftly towards the castle, and she could feel the anxiety knocking at her breast. A bee sting could be serious, and she felt certain it had touched the very corner of his eye and in a very short while the eye would be swollen and very painful.

CHAPTER EIGHT

LISE told herself that Leandro looked suitably piratic with a dark patch over his left eye, for the sting had left him looking as if he had been in a fight and he wore the patch in order to spare his grandmother the swollen, bloodshot appearance of the eye.

On the Saturday of that week Chano was returning to Madrid, and it was at breakfast on the *patio* that Leandro announced his intention of driving there with Chano, in order, he added, to clear up a business matter that could no' longer be left in abeyance. He would return to the *castillo* on Tuesday by hired car.

'Leandro, may I come as well?' Suddenly for Lise this seemed a way out of her predicament. In Madrid they could pretend to quarrel, and Leandro could return alone to inform his grandmother that the engagement was off. It all fitted so smoothly. He could tell the Condesa that she had found it imposssible to live in the country. He could ease out the hook without hurting anyone too deeply, for Lise was hopeful that once she was apart from him she would soon forget him. She could no longer remain in Spain, of course. Seeing other lean, dark Latin men would only keep reminding her of the Conde, and it would be better if she went home to England to forget.

She watched as he spread butter on a piece of toast, his gaze made even more inscrutable by reason of the dark patch. 'I don't think that it would be quite fair for both of us to leave Madrecita alone,' he said at last. 'Has not Ana told you that she is coming to Madrid to be presented to Chano's parents?'

'Yes, but I don't see what difference it makes? Manuela is here and your grandmother keeps to her apartment most of the time. Anyway, I can go in my own car now it's been repaired. You can't stop me.'

'Just listen to the girl, Chano.' The Conde drawled the words. 'Are you not glad that you are going to become engaged to a Spanish girl? At least they are a little more obedient.'

Chano gave a laugh and glanced across the table at Ana, who was demurely smiling as she ate her breakfast. 'But really, Leandro, I don't see why you insist that Lise remain behind while you enjoy a weekend in Madrid? I am sure the Condesa would not wish your *novia* to be deprived of a little pleasure.'

'You might remember, Chano, that I am going to Madrid on business.' Leandro spoke with a sudden ring of iron in his voice, and in that instant Lise felt sure that he intended to see Franquista. Her own heart hardened against him, and that traitorous softness of the past few days, stemming from her sympathy, was replaced by a flash of temper.

'I wouldn't dream of interfering with your little bit of business,' she said cuttingly. 'I'm quite sure it's of the ultimate importance to you, and I could only be in your way. I do see that, very clearly.'

'Then you agree to stay at the *castillo* until my return?' His right eye was boring into her, drilling her with its jetty darkness.

'I suppose so.' Lise bent her head and continued with her breakfast, and knew inevitably that she was going to have to get off the hook the painful way. Her car had been returned from the garage and was now in running order again, and much as she disliked the idea of causing distress to the Condesa, it could not be helped. She would leave a note to say that she couldn't bear the thought of living in Spain so many miles from her brother and his family. She would drive away and not look back, and when Leandro came home on Tuesday his grandmother would have accepted the situation, and Lise would not be around to face his anger.

She peeled an orange and made herself seem wholly interested in Ana and Chano, who in the past week had come fully alive to the fact that they were in love. Chano wished to make her his wife as soon as possible, and that was why Ana was going to Madrid with him, where his mother and father lived in a villa on the outskirts of the city. They had to be informed, and their blessing received, and Lise stifled a tiny sigh of envy.

'You're an awfully lucky girl,' she told Ana, and she said it in such a heartfelt way that Chano gave her a stare of pure amazement. He had come to believe like everyone else that the Conde was going to marry her, no doubt because Manuela had hinted at passionate embraces among the bougainvillea, and Lise could have laughed or wept at the painful memory of being kissed to stifle her mouth rather than being kissed because a man desired enjoyment of her lips.

'Being an English girl, Lise is just a tiny bit cynical,' Leandro put in smoothly. 'The tale of Cinderella is popular in her country because of Buttons rather than the Prince. Buttons is always the hero, while the noble scion is invariably played by a young woman, so making it ultimately unbelievable that the pair ever arrive at the altar. Lise can see Ana as a bride, but she cannot imagine herself in the same role, and all because I am not Buttons. Chano, you are an awfully lucky fellow.'

They all laughed at the droll way he spoke; even Lise caught her breath on a little laughter, and then she glanced away from his face because the love inside her hurt a little too much in that moment. If she married him this would be how she felt each time he returned to Madrid. She would know who drew him there, who held him there, until he was ready to come home once more to his Cinderella bride. It would be more endurable to be apart from him than to be the wife he didn't love.

After breakfast Ana and Chano went off to prepare for the journey, but Leandro lingered so that he might have a few private words with Lise, who knew the gist of them before he spoke.

He took her by the elbow and led her into one of the formal rooms off the hall, and he closed the door very firmly on their privacy. Lise put a hand to her throat and she looked everywhere but at the dark features that no longer smiled. The room to which he had brought her was distinctive and very Spanish, with its mosaic-tiled ceiling supported with such grace on fluted, dark marble pillars. There were high-backed chairs and cedar chests. Crimson curtains, candlesticks of gold, roses and a crucifix – an atmosphere of ritual, almost, for the roses were glowing like balls of flame in a golden chalice below the cross on the dark panelled wall. Beneath her toes was an immense vicuna rug, and above the mantelpiece was a portrait in a golden frame, of a woman with a clear olive-skinned face, huge dark, passionate eyes, and a full red, almost sulky mouth. Beside her mouth was the velvety dark mole of a truly sensuous woman, and on a chain about her neck ... Lise caught her breath, for the woman in the portrait was wearing the sapphire heart which Leandro had given *her* to wear.

She looked at him then, and he slowly raised a sardonic eyebrow, as if to let her know that he read her mind.

'The Brazilian bride of a former Marcos Reyes,' he said. 'I believe I told you about her ... the sapphire came from the jungles of Brazil and was carved to the shape of a heart in a Spanish workshop. Now and then it has been worn by a happy bride, for who am I to say that the men of this family are easy to get along with. However, my grandmother was happy in her marriage, and who can blame her if she wishes the same for me?'

'No one,' Lise murmured. 'But to find happiness it is surely best to marry for love.'

'I agree with you,' he said smoothly. 'Is it love, or is it *simpatia* of the heart, an expression which cannot be translated into English. It stands alone, wholly Latin; a thing of the soul and of the senses.'

'You know,' she moistened her lips, 'you really haven't much time in which to talk philosophy. Why did you bring me here?'

'I am sure you have already guessed.' And suddenly his face looked pitiless as he came towards her, so that she backed against one of the dark marble pillars and felt it cold against the grip of her hands. Her eyes were wide and grey in her pale face, and she had taken almost a crucified attitude against the pillar.

'I have to go to Madrid, and you have to stay here,' he said, and now he stood over her and she could see a tiny nerve tensely at work in his jaw. 'I know what is in your mind, *amiga*. As soon as my back is turned you plan to pack and run, and I am warning you that if you do so and Madrecita suffers as a consequence, I shall come after you, no matter where you are, and I shall make it my business to make you suffer. Do you believe me?'

'Yes,' she said faintly. 'But, Leandro, if I came with you to Madrid we could pretend to quarrel there and then we'd have a way out of this – this muddle, and you'd be free to – to live your own life.'

'You stay here at the *castillo*,' he said again, and his lips looked firm as iron around the words. 'When I told Madrecita that I was returning to Madrid for a few days, she made me promise that you would remain behind at El

Serafin. She became quite agitated, which means that she has become fond of you and now looks forward to having you – anyway, as you say there is no time for a fuller talk, just enough time for me to warn you that while I'm away you will not do something that I could never forgive.'

Abruptly, as he said these words, his hands gripped the pillar at either side of her head, and his look of menace was aggravated by the patch over his left eye. 'You quiver like an arrow in a bow,' he said quietly. 'You long to be released so that you can fly away, and because I know this I have removed from your car, and from the other two that stand in the garage, a tiny part of the mechanism that renders all the rest incapable of movement. I only wish, *pequeña*, that I could have trusted you, but as I can't, as I know you will behave like an irrational child—'

'It's exactly like you to behave like an arrogant, bossy lord of the manor,' she broke in, hating him for his distrust of her, and for his assumption that he and his grandmother could make a prisoner of her and force her to do what they wanted. 'I hate you, Leandro! And I know who you are going to see in Madrid!'

'I am sure you do,' he drawled, and with a mocking little laugh he deliberately bent his head and his kiss brushed across her furiously turned face.

'Keep your kisses for *her*!' Lise choked the words. 'They disgust *me*!'

'What a pity,' he drawled. 'And now what shall I bring you from Madrid? Perfume, bonbons, or perhaps a fur?'

'Keep your presents as well! Give them to *her*, as you plan to give yourself!'

'You seem very sure of my plans,' he said, and swift and lethal his fingers were at her chin, gripping it and forcing her face into line with his own. 'If you were a woman grown I'd say your female intuition was at work, but as you behave rather more like a child — oh yes, my little Doña Immaculata! If you were truly adult, you would understand a man a little better; if you were less quick to take temper and more composed, as a woman should be, you would not condemn so wildly.'

'I'm sure,' she panted, 'I'm everything *she* is not. It must be terribly frustrating for you that your grandmother can't see eye to eye with you over this matter of a wife. I can understand all right why you need to go haring off to Madrid, *señor*. I'm not that childish!'

Colour was stormy in her cheeks as she flung these words at him, and her fair hair was flung across her brow from the wild turning of her head. Her young breast rose and fell under the thin material of her shirt, and something of her inner torment was beginning to show itself. He had to go . . . go now, before she howled like a kid that he was going, leaving her at the castle while he went to Franquista.

'For heaven's sake don't waste another precious minute on me,' she said, coldly.

'You will be here when I return?' His fingers dug into her chin, making her wince.

'You've made sure of that, haven't you? You've put my car out of action, and played on my good will with regard to the Condesa. I—I like her, and I only wish—'

'Yes, *pequeña*? What do you wish?' A quizzical light seemed to come into his uninjured eye.

'I wish to heaven I could tell her the truth and end all this!'

'You will keep the truth to yourself,' he snapped. 'If you say one word about the true state of your feelings with regard to me, and cause Madrecita a shock to her heart, then I will break your lily-white neck.' And to emphasize his words he placed both hands about Lise's neck and forced back her head until her senses felt as if they were whirling.

Then he let her go and she stood clutching the marble pillar for support, and still felt the warm, hard impress of her fingers against her neck. She stared at him and realized that he was as emotionally churned up as herself . . . all the fury and the frustration smouldering in him, running molten through his veins, and just about ready to overwhelm someone.

He backed away from her and she knew that he was controlling himself with an effort.

'I am now going to say *hasta la vista*, Lise. You will not come to the car – I don't wish Ana or Chano to see how you hate me at this moment. Take good care of Madrecita, and expect me back on Tuesday.'

He walked to the door, opened it and gave her a brief inclination of the head. 'Are you not going to say farewell to me?'

'I am sure you will fare well, Señor Conde.' She forced a cold insolence into her voice. 'And please don't insult me by bringing back a gift of perfume or chocolates . . . and as for fur, I would never wear it, because I don't like cruelty.'

'*Muy bien, amiga.*' His gaze flicked her figure from head to foot, and then he was gone and the door was closed, and there wasn't a sound in that crimson-curtained room . . . until all at once Lise gave a sob and buried her face in her hands.

The castle seemed very quiet after the car had left with its three occupants. After bathing her face in cold water, and combing her hair into a clasp at the nape of her neck, Lise went down to the stables and asked the groom who was in charge to saddle her a mount. She felt a stifled need to get away from the castle for a while, and if she couldn't have the use of her car, she would ride one of the horses.

'*Si, señorita,*' said Juan. 'The horse of Señorita Ana is

well-behaved and she would like him to be exercised while she is away.'

Lise nodded, and also bit her lip, for it hurt such a lot that she had been left alone here while those three went to Madrid, all on missions of love.

Jacinto, the sleek black horse which Ana looked so well on, wearing the divided skirt, soft white shirt frilled at the front, and hard-brimmed Cordoban hat tilted at an angle above her dark eyes, was used to a slim, light rider, but Lise and he were soon used to each other and as soon as he snuffed the sea, for which she was heading down the gradual slope of the cliffs, he jingled his harness and trotted at a lively pace.

Upon reaching the lonely stretch of beach they galloped, splashing through the waves that ebbed and flowed along the edge of the sands. The sun glittered on the water, and far out Lise could glimpse the rock to which she had swum that morning Leandro had saved her when cramp had gripped her leg.

Was that when she had fallen in love with him? There was no sense in evading the truth any longer . . . she loved the man, and that was why she had cried when he had left her alone in that room, there beneath the portrait of the Brazilian girl wearing the blue stone heart. Lise had never cried over a man before; she had never dreamed that love could be an actual physical ache. Her eyes shimmered again as she gazed ahead at the long serpentine of pale gold sand, pierced here and there by the dark rocks, some of which were mantled with blue-green seaweeds.

The lonely sands and the rocks, and the sea whispering and sobbing, were so evocative of her mood that Lise felt like staying here for hours, but if she did so, and her absence was noticed, they would become anxious at the castle, and she couldn't forget the look there had been on Leandro's face

168

when he had warned her not to upset the Condesa by attempting to run away while he was absent.

She brought the horse to a halt and sat still in the saddle and took a deep steadying breath of the sea air, filling her eyes and her lungs with it in an attempt to dispel her melancholy. Above the sea rolled clouds like great golden dragons and she wondered for a moment if there was going to be a storm. Somehow she would welcome the crash of thunder and the hiss of lightning, flashing round the castle and shaking the ancient walls.

Perhaps if Leandro heard of the storm while he was in Madrid he would be a little anxious, even guilty that he raked off seeking the pleasure of Franquista's company, knowing all the time that she was a woman intensely disapproved of by his grandmother.

Lise gripped the reins as she pictured him with his arms around the Latin woman, who would not thrust him away, or struggle, or tell him childishly to let her go. She would smile and offer him those red and luscious lips. She would warmly enclose him with her creamy arms and allow her fingers to caress the nape of his neck . . . and being a man that was what he wanted and needed – not the puerile behaviour of a girl who reacted to him as if he were a villain.

The trouble was . . . a sigh shook her. Oh, she knew what lay at the root of her reactionary behaviour. It wasn't enough to be kissed, or thought of as pretty enough to produce the next heir to the castle . . . she wanted Leandro to be as shaken by love of her as she was shaken by love of him. It wasn't enough to have him for a husband, not if he gave only his body and not his heart. It wasn't heaven which he offered; it was only a castle in Spain and a life made easy, instead of a life made electrical with love triggered off by a look, a brush of hands, a flash of words, a softly molten smile.

The dragon-shaped clouds swam lower over the sea, and as the horse jibbed with sudden restlessness, Lise felt certain that she caught a murmur of thunder above the *sierras*.

'Come on, boy,' she said. 'Let's go back.'

The shining hooves churned the sand, and the sea wind blew over Lise's brow and throat, tossing her hair from her neck and catching the golden motes in it. When she and her mount trotted into the courtyard, there was colour in her cheeks, a sea-blaze in her eyes, and she looked for all the world like a girl who hadn't a care at heart.

When suddenly she caught sight of the Condesa, taking lemon tea and biscuits beneath the colonnade of the patio, she brought Jacinto to a halt and called out a greeting.

Leandro's grandmother gazed at her in silence for several moments, taking in her fairness against the sleek darkness of the horse. 'Hullo, my child. You must come and join me in a glass of tea.'

'I should like that.' Lise smiled involuntarily, for the Condesa looked such a marvel for her age, seated there in a chair of woven cane with a high fan back, wearing a lilac-coloured dress, and a mantilla of cobweb-lace over her perfectly groomed silver hair. There were tiny jewels in the lobes of her ears, diamonds glittering about her wrists, and her feet in small, shining shoes were perched on a footstool. A newspaper lay at her elbow, and a lorgnette moved in her fingers like a fan. She looked as if she ought to be painted, but Lise knew that the tedium of sitting for the portrait would have exhausted both her strength and her patience.

'How lovely you look, *señora*.' The words broke with shy sincerity from Lise, who then trotted Jacinto to his stall and left him in the care of the groom.

'You had a good ride, *señorita*?' Juan gave her the respectful but slightly indulgent smile she was beginning to expect from the Conde's staff. It was as if they found her young and strange but quite *guapa* as the prospective bride; almost as good as a Latin girl. She did not put on airs or try to humble them, and as she gazed into Juan's dark and leathery face, she could have wept at their trust in Leandro. They believed in him as she couldn't. Good, strong, sensual people that they were, they thought he loved her. They approved his choice of a fresh and innocent girl, for like the Condesa they were old-fashioned and would have been shocked had he brought to the castle a divorced woman as his future wife.

'I had an excellent ride, Juan,' she smiled. 'Along by the sea – but I noticed there were clouds about. Are we in for some rain?'

'Much rain, *señorita*. Perhaps a storm.' The groom gave her a gravely amused but searching look. 'You don't fear storms, eh? Not the *novia* of *el señor*?'

'I should hope not.' She gave a laugh as she took the deeper meaning in his words; it wouldn't do for any woman involved with the Conde to be afraid of the elements. She caressed the velvety nose of Jacinto, and then went quickly indoors, and up to her rooms to change from trousers to her lemon-flowered chiffon. This was a concession to the Condesa, who considered that trousers were unbecoming on a woman. Lise combed out her hair and left it loose on her shoulders, and with rather solemn eyes she studied her reflection in the mirror. Her cheeks were still flushed from her ride and she had a fresh and charming look. She bit her lip and was vaguely confused that she could have this look of a girl in love when in her heart she knew that love to be doomed. Nothing lasting could come of what she felt for the Conde, for she did not intend to go through with this impossible marriage.

Nothing could persuade her short of a declaration of love from him, and that would not be forthcoming.

The soft chiffon swirled about her slim legs as she turned from the mirror and left her bedroom. She made her way quickly down the stairs and went out to join the Condesa under the cool cloisters, where a tangle of blue columbine drooped, spilling their sweet coolness to the tiles.

While she had been absent the Condesa had wrung the little silver bell and a plate of cream cakes had been brought to the table, along with a little jug of cream. 'I know you prefer your tea in the English way.' The old lady gave Lise an approving look. 'I believe that in the time you have been with us, child, you have become so charming as to be called lovely. To Latin eyes, you know, the fair skin and hair of the Anglo-Saxon is most refreshing. I am pleased with you. I think that you and Leandro between you will make fine and spirited children.' And then the Condesa chuckled as the flush deepened in Lise's cheeks, and she busied herself with the little velvet bag in her hand while Lise poured out a cup of tea and battled for composure. Such personal comments seemed to draw her ever deeper into the plot from which, somehow, she had to disentangle herself.

'Please help yourself to cakes, child. They are made from an old Moorish recipe which has been in the family for years. The Moors were always fond of sweet things, and I am sure you have guessed, or been informed by Leandro, that the Marcos Reyes have a dash of the Moor in their veins. All the most handsome men of Spain have this strain in them.' And with these words the Condesa opened the velvet bag and took from it a small object that caught the sun and sparkled madly. 'I wish you to have this trinket, child, because it was given to me with great love. Hold open your hand!'

Lise could not refuse to do so, and the next instant the object sparkled in her palm and she was staring at the perfectly wrought love-knot set with diamonds and small gleaming rubies.

'Passion and warmth, child. Two of the ingredients so essential when it comes to love.'

'It's beautiful, *señora*, perfect, but I—'

'If you dare to say that you cannot accept it, then you and I will have words. I want you to have the brooch, and you will give me the pleasure of pinning it on your dress; there above your heart where it belongs.'

'You really are too kind.' Lise's hand shook slightly as she pinned the love-knot into place, for like a real knot it seemed to bind her ever closer in relationship to this family. Oh God, not that she wouldn't have gloried in those bonds, had they been bonds of love and desire; a true warmth of passion instead of a sham.

'The brooch looks very pretty, child, and you must promise me you will wear it on the day you marry—' There, to the intense relief of Lise, the Condesa broke off her words as a manservant came to her elbow with a letter salver. Both Lise and the Condesa stared at the blue envelope, and Lise recalled that other letter on blue paper, in which that friend of the Condesa's had gossiped about Leandro's association with Franquista.

What now? Lise wondered.

'*Gracias.*' The ringed fingers took the letter and Lise could see it shaking slightly as the Condesa studied the handwriting. Then as the manservant walked away and disappeared inside the castle, there came a ripping sound as Leandro's grandmother deliberately tore the unopened letter into pieces.

'It is a strange fact, Lise, that one's friends can sometimes be too well-meaning. My old friend in Madrid means to do me a service by letting me know about the women who chase after Leandro, but I no longer need to be put into that particular picture. Also it would upset me to be reminded that he—' she spread her jewelled hands. 'He is *tiene buena sombra, tiene gracia*, so naturally there have been these women to amuse him. That is now all over—'

There she checked herself and stared at Lise, who had reached so blindly for the milk jug that she had upset it. Hastily she mopped up with a table napkin, before the milk could spill from the table on to her dress.

'What is the matter?' The Condesa leaned forward and gripped Lise's hand. Her fingernails dug into the flesh, but she seemed unaware of this, of the pain and alarm she sent shooting through Lise.

'I – I'm clumsy, Madrecita. Still a little excited by your gift—'

'No, there is something else! Has Leandro gone to Madrid to see this woman who was divorced from her husband?'

'No—'

'You will tell me the truth!' The Condesa's fingers gripped remorselessly, pressing into Lise her rings and her fear. 'I am not so old and frail that I cannot be told the truth – for once. Come, my child, I can tell from your face that you know the real reason why he has gone there and I insist that you tell me what you know.'

'I – I know very little, *señora*. I merely suspected that he might go to see her, as she is an old friend, and a business associate—'

'Business associate, that *mujer inconstante? Por Dios*, and knowing he was going to *her*, you let him go, child! When I was your age I could have held back a man, especially a man I loved. Ah, don't flinch from the truth, *menina*. I know you love the wretch.'

'Do you also know, *señora*, that he doesn't love me?'

'Bah, I have seen you in his arms. He desires you, and a clever girl can always turn that to her advantage. This other

174

one – he knows I will not have her under my roof. I will not permit the Marcos Reyes name to pass to a woman who has already gone through a form of marriage with another man. She is unchaste—' Abruptly the Condesa let go of Lise's hand and lay back in her chair with an exhausted look on her face. 'I am allowing myself to become agitated and it is not good for my old heart. Lise, I must have your promise that you will marry Leandro. He has given you his ring, his promise, and he knows very well that all his people at El Serafin are eager for the moment when the hawk mates with the dove. They expect the *bianca paloma* for their young *condesa*, not the scarlet woman! They expect the virgin bride there at the altar on his arm ... the lily, not the orchid!'

'Please, *señora*, you must not upset yourself.' Lise hastened round the table to the side of the Condesa and the last remnants of her shyness were scattered as she put her arms around the lovely proud, frail woman and softly kissed her face. 'Leandro will do his duty, you know that, Madrecita. He will not let you down – nor will I, if I can help it.'

Manuela, who was never far away, came hurrying from the shadow of the cloisters in that moment. She and Lise between them assisted the Condesa to her apartment on the ground floor, and after Lise had made sure that Leandro's grandmother was all right, merely tired after her upset, she made her way to the Conde's study where she took an English edition of *Wuthering Heights* from the shelf and sat in the deep window seat to read of Heathcliff's passionate and terrible love for Catherine. *Monster! would that he could be blotted out of creation, and out of my memory!*

After reading those desperate words Lise gazed from the window and saw the day going sultry, the colour of those clouds that had swum in from the sea and were now banked above the turrets of the castle. Juan had predicted a storm, and once again Lise had that feeling that she wanted thunder and lightning and a clearing of the air.

She was still sitting there with the book in her lap, alternating her gaze from the window to the words *Together, they would brave Satan and all his legions*, when the door opened and Florentina surged into the room.

'So here you are in *his* room, dreaming and feeling a bit blue. But you must eat some lunch, and I have come to ask what you would like.'

'Oh, anything will do. I am not really hungry—'

'A *menina* with a man on her mind is rarely hungry, but that is no reason why you should sit here and starve. A Spaniard expects a bride who feels like a woman in his arms, not a broomstick. Come now,' the big smile grew on Florentina's face, 'how about *para picar*, eh? A little of sliced sausage, some of my honey-baked ham, a bit of cheese, a tomato and cucumber in vinegar? Tasty, eh? To wake up the hunger buds.'

'How can I resist?' Lise broke into a smile. 'I'll have it here beside me because I like the view from this window.'

'*Muy bueno.*' Florentina looked knowing. 'And one can smell the cigars that have been smoked here, and there is nothing more provoking to the memory than the scent of a man's cigar. I will bring gingerbread as well. I have just baked some and it is good straight from the oven – always from a boy the *señor conde* liked to come to my kitchen for hot gingerbread.'

'I always thought,' murmured Lise, 'that someone was responsible for the ginger in him.'

'What is a man without it?' Florentina chuckled, and then glanced about the leather-lined study. 'But are you sure you will eat here? The room has a certain gloom today, and the figures in that tapestry seem to move to my mind.'

'It's only an illusion caused by a draught,' said Lise,

gazing herself at the *conquistadores* in their gleaming casques and armoured vests. 'I rather like them, for they look as if nothing could ever humble them. They are so Spanish, so very proud and armoured.'

Lise shot a smile at Florentina, but in answer she received a rather serious look, one which took in her youthful hair-style, her pale dress, and her legs tucked beneath her as she sat there in the windowseat framed by the long velvet curtains.

'Stand up to him.' Florentina spoke abruptly. 'Don't be meek or saintly, as his mother was!'

The door closed behind the large figure in the rustling dress and apron, but her words lingered in the room and they made Lise realize how tightly the trap of this expected marriage was closing around her. Her struggles for release seemed to entangle her ever deeper in the lives and hopes of the people at El Serafin. Because the castle was so isolated, so relatively untouched by the modern ways, the old values still held sway. Leandro was the master here, but still he owed it to his people, and most of all to his grandmother, to provide a virgin bride . . . the true and authentic sacrifice to the pagan laws of love.

Lise sat pensive in the windowseat, feeling the weight of the loveknot above the heaviness of her heart. How quickly beat her heart, while her thoughts flew along the road to Madrid. They would arrive some time in the evening, for Chano was a fast driver. Leandro would go to his apartment there, while Ana would go home with Chano, happy in the glowing knowledge that she was loved and wanted for herself.

The sapphire gleamed darkly on Lise's hand as she clenched the curtain beside her, crushing the velvet as a tormenting vision arose in her mind of Leandro speaking on the telephone to Franquista, arranging to meet her, possibly at a smart, softly lit restaurant where they would discuss their problem and later come to terms with it at her apartment. They were worldly people who would find a way to adjust to a relationship which must include a third person . . . herself.

A tremor ran through Lise, for it was she who could not adjust to the idea of sharing Leandro with another woman. She closed her eyes as the remorseless truth swept over her . . . she wanted all of him, or none of him. Somehow the trap in which she found herself must be sprung . . . she would write to her sister-in-law and between them they would plot a way for her to get back to England without causing harm to the Condesa. Once there, safely away from Leandro, the days could slip into weeks until finally she was forgotten.

That was the way it must be . . . she would not, could not contemplate a marriage that would suit everyone but herself. She wasn't that meek or that saintly.

The heavy rains began to fall late that afternoon, seeming to drive down from the peaks like lances of silver, blotting out the landscape and pounding on the trees and flowers so that Lise felt sure many of them would be driven to the ground to lie there draggled and wet until they perished. She thought of the bougainvillea which so loved the hot sun, and the fragile columbines that would never hold their own in such a fierce onslaught.

All the lights were lit in the castle as the storm intensified, and Lise went without being asked to the apartment of the Condesa to make certain she wasn't unnerved by the tumult of rain and the hiss of the lightning through the black clouds, striking at the windows and playing around the turrets like dark red fire. The thunder seemed to echo back and forth among the peaks of the mountains, and Lise gave a jump as Manuela opened the door to her at the same moment a heavy crack of thunder echoed along the corridor.

'The Condesa,' Lise's voice shook slightly, 'she is all right?'

'Of course, *señorita*.' Manuela smiled and beckoned Lise into the sitting-room of the suite. 'The Condesa has lived in this part of the world for most of her life and she is accustomed to these storms that come during the hot weather. What of you, *señorita*? You are not yet accustomed to them.'

'I must confess that I find this particular storm a bit terrifying.' Lise jumped again as the castle seemed to tremble in the grip of some giant fist. 'From the study I could hear the horses stamping and neighing, and suddenly I was anxious and felt like some company. May I sit with you, Manuela?'

'With pleasure, *señorita*. I am sewing beads on a headscarf and you can sew the other end, if you wish?'

'I wish.' Lise gave a shaky smile and glanced at the closed door of the Condesa's bedroom. 'Is she asleep, through all this?'

'She has had a small sedative and will sleep for a while longer.' Manuela gave Lise a steady look, her dark eyes both curious and concerned. 'I know that the *señora* received a letter from Madrid this morning. Was it that which upset her? She has so set her mind on the Conde's nuptial happiness that the slightest whisper of doubt ... *señorita*, I don't mean to pry, but there were strong rumours at one time that the Conde had an attachment to a – another woman. I think we all fear that she will in some way come between—' Manuela broke off and bit her lip. Then she hurried on: 'Men are not always as true and loyal as women ... some, perhaps, but not all, and it is well known that the Conde's father was unfaithful to that kind, good creature whom he married straight from a convent. These instincts are in the blood, and the Condesa knows this and always she is in fear that history will repeat itself. Now he has gone off – you understand, *señorita*, it is not that storm out there that can harm the Condesa. It is the inner storm. She said to me today – you do not mind that I speak frankly?'

Lise shook her head and sat down in the chair which Manuela indicated. The windows shook as she did so, and she heard the rain splashing down on the flagstones of the courtyard, on the coloured tiles of the patio, that would be awash with rainwater, and the petals of flowers.

Manuela had lit a fire and the warmth was agreeable as Lise leant to the flames and held her hands to the glow.

The Condesa's companion sat down in a basket chair and the beaded scarf glittered in her fingers as she took it up again. 'The English woman,' she said, 'is not so well trained in patience or obedience to the whims of a man. The Condesa fears that you will not marry the Conde if he continues to see this other woman.'

'She has said so, Manuela?' Lise didn't glance from the flames, for they seemed to writhe around the logs in a similar agony to her inner feelings.

'Yes, she confessed this to me, for we are close, you understand.' Manuela dropped a bead and left it to lie on the rug. Her gaze was fixed upon Lise's profile in the firelight. 'He has gone to see her, has he not?'

'I believe so.' Lise spoke quietly, but inwardly she was torn apart by the certainty that soon he would be with Franquista, leaving *her* to carry the burden of his grandmother's peace of mind. Leaving it up to her to assure the Condesa that she would go through with this marriage come what may.

How dared he do that? How dared he be so sure that the material things he offered would outweigh her natural desire for that most elusive thing of all . . . the love that could be felt but never grasped . . . the love that shot from one soul to the other, like lightning through the dark, forging with fire a bond that only death could sever.

How dared Leandro suppose that she would cower before his threats, and be here on Tuesday to feel on her hand, her body, the touch that all the weekend had been Franquista's!

'Manuela,' Lise sat up very straight in her chair and looked across at the companion, who probably knew the Condesa better than anyone else,' 'do you think the *señora* could bear to be told that I – that I wish to break my engagement to the Conde?'

In the silence that followed the thunder seemed to deepen, to penetrate more deeply the environs of the castle.

'I – I keep being forced into promises which I can't keep,' Lise went on. 'It seems that everyone matters except me. That everyone's feelings must be considered except mine. It's as if I'm a puppet instead of a person; as if I'm filled with straw instead of feelings. If I had no feelings I wouldn't be concerned for the Condesa, and it's that concern alone which keeps me here. I know her heart is weak, but is it so weak that she would suffer collapse if a mere English girl walked out and left a note to say that she can't live in Spain, that it's too far from her family in England? Would she not understand and forgive me?'

'Very possibly,' said Manuela. 'But would the Conde forgive you if the blow to her hopes was too much for her?'

'Do you believe that it would be too much of a blow?'

'I am not a doctor, *señorita*, but I do know that she had set her heart on this one thing, possibly the last strong wish she will have on this earth. She fears, you see, that if you do not marry him, then he will marry this other woman. Not yet, of course. Not while she lives, but some day inevitably.'

'Oh God!' Lise clasped her hands together. 'He has no right to do this to me. I was a stranger to him, that night my car broke down and he brought me here and talked me into posing as his *novia*. I thought it would last only a week or so . . . I never dreamed it would come to this. It's become like a nightmare from which I can't wake up—'

'But I am glad that I woke up,' said a voice by the bedroom door. 'I am glad I have heard the truth at last.'

Lise leapt to her feet, while Manuela's box of tiny beads fell from her lap and rolled in all directions. Together they stared at the Condesa, who stood just in the doorway of her bedroom, holding around her a robe of purple brocade.

'It is, of course, a pity,' she said, 'for you have the spirit to have made him a good wife. However, you cannot be forced against your will to go through with a masquerade to the very steps of the altar. I will arrange that in the morning you are driven to the nearest airport and from there you can book a flight home to England. I am sure, my child, that you will wish to go while Leandro is away from home. You will not wish to see again this devil who has forced you into playing such a false role. You must hate him – perhaps almost as much as you reluctantly love him.'

Then, as Lise still stood there stunned, the Condesa made her way to a window and for several moments she watched the slashing rain and the flashing lightning. 'The gods are in a rage,' she murmured. 'Who can blame them, when men and women will play with love as if it were a toy instead of a living element to be treated with reverence? Manuela, I think we could all do with a glass of wine to soothe our shaken nerves. And, Lise, my child, do stop looking at me as if I am about to fall into fragments, like the old parchment I am. I am more annoyed over all this than shocked. As a grandson of mine I gave Leandro credit for preferring gold to dross, but if he cannot safeguard his gold once it is in his hands, and prefers to gamble with it, then he has only himself to blame if he ends up a bankrupt at the court of love.'

The storm lasted well into the night, and it might have been just after midnight when Lise turned over in bed and thought she heard voices down in the courtyard. She raised herself on her elbow and wondered what could be wrong. Suddenly, with anxiety clutching at her, she slipped out of bed, pulled on her robe, pushed her feet into her slippers and went out on to the veranda. She saw light streaming out from one of the ground-floor rooms, and had the sudden dread thought that the doctor had been called to attend to the Condesa. As a spot of rain fell on to her cheek from the stonework above where she stood, she turned and hastened from her bedroom and made her way to the stairs. She had almost reached the hall when someone came out of the *sala*, a tall figure stripped to white shirt and dark trousers, black hair agleam as if only recently it had been wet with the rain.

'Leandro!' His name broke from Lise, and she was so startled that she tripped on the stairs and only just saved herself by clutching at the wrought-iron balustrade. Her heart was in her throat somewhere, and then he was coming up the stairs to her. His arms went round her and he lifted her as if she had been a child and carried her down to the room from which he had emerged . . . a dark and very vital being.

'Why aren't you there, in Madrid?' Lise stared at him with huge grey eyes, while still he held her in his arms, until suddenly he gave the door a kick and it closed behind them and they were alone together in the *sala*, where his coat was slung to a chair, and where his cases stood, spattered with raindrops.

'Would you sooner I were in Madrid?' he asked, and very lazily his good eye travelled down her slim neck to the opening of her robe, where pale nylon moved rapidly up and down with her startled breathing. 'Do you not prefer to have me here, *mi amiga*?'

'But I don't understand, *señor*.' She stared at his face, so dark, so close to her, wearing the slightly wicked smile of the devil she was going to escape when morning came. 'Where is Ana, and Chano? What happened?'

'They continued on their way to their destination, *matadora*. I returned to face my destiny.' Slowly he allowed Lise to fall to her feet, but still he kept his arms around her, holding her slim, night-clad figure against him. 'We stopped on the road to take lunch and when I looked back I saw how stormy the sky looked. I told our two friends to continue their journey, while I would remain at the inn to arrange for a car to bring me back to the castle.'

'All because of a storm?' Lise murmured. 'But you were on your way to see Fránquista. What could be more important than that?'

'That you might get away from me before I had a chance – ah, you gave a jump just then, which tells me that you were going away, regardless of my threats.'

'I am still going—' She tried to pull free of him, but as always he was too strong for her and she had to stay still or be bruised against him. 'I mean it, Leandro. Your grandmother knows everything—'

'*Santo Dios*, you did not dare—?'

'No, she overheard me in conversation with Manuela.' I had to talk to someone – but she took it so well, and she is going to arrange that I leave the *castillo* for good, in the morning.'

'Really?' His tone was so mild, but when Lise looked at his mouth she saw that it was edged with temper. 'So on

Tuesday I was to return to find you gone … and every single singing bird as silent as the grave! Every bit of sunlight like a shadow.'

'Leandro?' Lise spoke faintly. 'I'm not with you, but I truly thought you were going to Madrid to be with—'

'Shut up!' he said rudely. 'And listen! In my time I have known several women, and Franquista was certainly one of them. She was gay, sparkling and clever, and we did business together, and sometimes we went to the bullfight and she adored nothing better than being given the ears and the tail of the brave bull. I know what you believed about her in connection with me, and it suited my purpose to let you think that I was in love with her. Had you guessed for one moment that I had no intention of loving anyone but you — yes, *matadora*, you — then in a virginal flurry of panic you would have fled me. You would never have believed the truth, that I wanted you for yourself and not for any other reason. You are such an independent, very British little creature, that if I had told you that our engagement was never for one moment a sham on my side, you would have scorned the very idea that a man can take one look at a woman and know she is the only woman for him. It is a fallacy that the female of the species is more romantic than the male. From the moment I brought you to my castle I meant to keep you here. You fitted into my plans so well. You fitted into my heart so perfectly. And in my arms you felt so slim, so adorable.'

In his arms, shaken and weak, Lise felt like hitting him for the torment he had put her through. 'Y-you blackmailed me,' she accused. 'You said I had to marry you for the sake of your grandmother. You set such a trap for me that all I wanted was to get out of it.'

'Yes,' he said thoughtfully. 'I went a bit too far, didn't I? You will have to forgive me for that, *guapissima*.'

185

'I won't,' she stormed. 'You've behaved like a – a devil and you don't deserve to be loved—'

'Loved?' he whispered, bending close to her. 'Loved, my lily, by you? Kissed by you, wanted by you, eared and tailed like the bull itself, my *matadora*.'

'Stop it!' She thrust a hand against his shoulder. 'You can't say you're going to see Franquista, and then come here to me with all this talk about – about loving me.'

'It was you, my little bit of fire, who said I was going to see Franquista. No doubt I would have seen her in Madrid, as she is seen everywhere, but the truth of the matter was that I was going to sign the agreement regarding our new factory, and as the papers are in the hands of the lawyer, I had naturally to go to his office, which is in Madrid. While there I planned to buy you this and that, but all the presents can wait. They can wait, my dear, but this can't!'

And swiftly, while her lips were still apart in surprise, he swooped and took them ... the hawk with the dove ... but a dove who was not tame to his hand, or likely to coo more often than she fought with him. She fought now, but the warmth, the hard, searching caress of his lips was too flamy sweet for resisting, and with her surrender came the true awakening to all he had said to her.

She was loved by him ... the lightning of the soul had flickered and they were forged as one. A feeling of quick-silver seemed to be running through her veins and her bones, while all the lovely images were alive in her mind as his lips took their pleasure of her. Soon in the cathedral at Jaen the candles would shine among the sprays of golden cassia; there would be a litany of bells, and the marriage vows would be read in beautiful Latin. That day the sun would blaze, and she would call him *esposo mio* ... husband mine!

Now available!

COLLECTION EDITIONS

of Harlequin Romances

Harlequin is proud to present this collection of the
best-selling romance novels of former years. This
is a rare series of 100 books, reissued in beautifully
designed new covers. And the cost is only 75¢
each. See complete listing on accompanying
pages.

Harlequin Collection Editions

Please note: The number in brackets indicates the original Harlequin Romance number.

Harlequin Collection Editions

Please note: The number in brackets indicates the original Harlequin Romance number.

Harlequin Collection Editions

Please note: The number in brackets indicates the original Harlequin Romance number.

Harlequin Collection Editions

Please note: The number in brackets indicates the original Harlequin Romance number.

Complete and mail this coupon today!